P9-DNU-809

AMERICAN DE

AN AMOS WALKER NOVEL

AMERICAN DETECTIVE

LOREN D. ESTLEMAN

THORNDIKE
CHIVERS

This Large Print edition is published by Thorndike Press, Waterville, Maine, USA, and by BBC Audiobooks Ltd, Bath, England.

Thorndike Press is an imprint of Thomson Gale, a part of The Thomson Corporation.

Thorndike is a trademark and used herein under license.

The text of this Large Print edition is unabridged.

Other aspects of the book may vary from the original edition.

Set in 16 pt. Plantin.

LIBRARY OF CONGRESS CATALOGING-IN-PUBLICATION DATA

Estleman, Loren D.
  American detective : an Amos Walker novel / by Loren D. Estleman.
    p. cm.
  ISBN-13: 978-0-7862-9683-5 (hardcover : alk. paper)
  ISBN-10: 0-7862-9683-6 (hardcover : alk. paper)
  1. Walker, Amos (Fictitious character) — Fiction. 2. Private investigators — Michigan — Detroit — Fiction. 3. Baseball players — Crimes against — Fiction. 4. Fathers and daughters — Fiction. 5. Detroit (Mich.) — Fiction. 6. Large type books. I. Title.
PS3555.S84A44 2007
813'.54—dc22   2007015520

BRITISH LIBRARY CATALOGUING-IN-PUBLICATION DATA AVAILABLE

Published in 2007 in the U.S. by arrangement with
Tom Doherty Associates, LLC.
Published in 2007 in the U.K. by arrangement with St. Martin's Press.

U.K. Hardcover: 978 1 405 64206 4 (Chivers Large Print)
U.K. Softcover: 978 1 405 64207 1 (Camden Large Print)

Printed in the United States of America on permanent paper
10 9 8 7 6 5 4 3 2 1

This book is dedicated to the memory
of Robin Lynch.
Heaven needed the humor.

ONE

The driveway was white stone, like a spill of salt between polished granite posts. A square of teal-colored lawn lay on either side, with furniture arranged on it in suites no decorator would approve: sectional sofas next to six-burner ranges, gold-plated bathroom fixtures among patio chairs carefully lichened with blobs of verdigris, stereo components deployed on top of plate-glass aquariums with no fish inside. A life-size statue of the property's owner cast in bronze stood on a carved mound with one foot raised, winding up to pitch a baseball. With a realtor's red-white-and-blue sign stuck in front of the quasi-neoclassical-Greco-Roman-Gothic-Art-Moderne house sprawled in the center of the lot, it was the most expensive yard sale since they put Soviet Russia on the block.

Small platoons of people, dressed casually and expensively but always appropriate to the blue eye of Lake St. Clair across the street, drifted from one set of objects to another, swigging from their personal bottles of water and commenting on the owner's taste or lack of it. I'd thought to take a drink from the tap before I left home, and so wandered empty-handed through spaces in between until I came to the statue. The baseball in the loose split-finger grip was real, common cowhide packed with horsehair and zipped up with thirty-three stitches, scuffed and dirty, with an illegible signature scrawled on it in indelible blue ink.

"Sculptor got it wrong," said the person who had stepped up from behind me, quiet as dew. "I knuckleballed the last three pitches in that game. But it looked too good to complain."

"That's the actual ball?" I asked.

"The one and only."

"Expensive setting."

"Not so much as the ball. I turned down a quarter million for it five years ago. How many no-hitters you see pitched by a man past forty?"

I turned his way then. Darius Fuller at sixty looked fit enough to suit up and open for the Tigers that afternoon. He was tall and rangy, with gray eyes in a thoughtful brown face that seemed to look down at me from a mound he carried around with him. His hair was a silver haze mowed close to his skull, but aside from that he could pass for thirty, which was still old for a ballplayer, and ancient for a hurler. He'd hung up the glove after that no-hitter at age forty-two, at the end of his third best season since he'd graduated from reliever to starter. The sportswriters had called him "the Fuller Brush Man" for the way he swept aside the top of the order.

He changed hands on a tall glass of something pale green and frosty and shook my hand. His grip was strong, with a punishing torque courtesy of a misshapen wrist — a feature not uncommon among longtime screwballers. It took a twist that turned the palm out when he let it hang at his side.

"You're Walker." He made it sound like the end of an argument.

I tipped my head toward the house. "Why couldn't I be an interested buyer?"

"You aren't dressed for it."

"It's a new suit."

"That's what I mean. Rich folks dress like shit. They got nobody to impress."

"You're dressed okay."

His navy polo shirt and putty-colored khakis fit him as snugly as the old uniform.

He had on hundred-dollar sneakers and a clump of gold and diamonds glittered on his left hand. He twisted it with his right without spilling his drink. "I'm po' folks now, ain't you heard? Everything today brings in goes straight to Uncle Sam. I done got traded from the private sector for three ex-wives and a business manager to be apprehended later."

"A lot of people would be bitter about it."

His face, which had stiffened with controlled rage, cracked apart then to let out a grin. He'd had a lot of work done on his teeth since he'd stopped a line drive with his mouth in '69. "Oh, hell," he said. "So I do a couple seasons of fantasy camp and slap my name on a ballpoint pen that writes under six feet of goose grease and split down the middle with D.C. Broke and famous aren't the same thing as being just plain broke."

"You should've taken the quarter million."

"It wouldn't pay the interest." He took a drink, watching me over the top of the glass. He appeared to be shaking off signals from the catcher, then nodded snappily and lowered the glass. "You're like a priest or a lawyer, right? Whatever I say stays with you."

"I look at it that way. The cops don't. I've been traded from the private sector a couple of times myself."

A short-haired blonde woman in shorts with a tennis bracelet came up on us holding a leather-bound book and a gold pen. He took them from her and twisted out the point. "This for you or a friend?"

"It's my checkbook. I want to buy the dining room set."

He stuck the items back at her. "You need to wait for the bidding, and then you don't pay me."

She left. He frowned. "What the hell was I saying?"

"Something about being broke but famous."

He'd started to raise his glass again. He lowered it. "You suck up to all your customers this way?"

"Sorry. I see a hole and I drive on through. It cost me a business degree."

"Don't apologize, it ruins it. A man that'll insult you to your face is a man that'll tell you the truth. I can tell you now I lied about that being the ball I threw in the no-hitter. I've got a dozen of them rolling around. When the auditor left I came damn close to selling every one as the ball and taking off for some island."

"What stopped you?"

"I can't swim and I don't tan."

I grinned.

He didn't. "Anyway, the real ball goes with me. Everything I ever bought may belong to the government, but the best moment in my career, that's mine and nobody else's. You can buy ten new suits with what they'll pay you to pass that on to them."

"My closet's only big enough for two and my gun. Where can we talk? Sound travels on the lake."

"The playhouse. It's out back."

I followed his long stride around an east wing held up by columns and walled with glass into a backyard with a crescent-shaped pool sunk in green tile. Keeping pace was a challenge; I was younger, but not by enough to make much difference, and I'd taken a bullet through my thigh last November that hadn't done anything for my running game. He unlocked the door to a miniature version of the house's center section, nine feet high and eleven wide, and let me into a room just big enough to stretch out in on the hardwood floor. The walls were hung with school pennants, pictures of a gangling teenage ballplayer in a succession of unfamiliar uniforms, and shelves of tall trophies with brass athletes writhing on top of them. The place smelled like old magazines and was built solider than my three-room refrigerator box in Hamtramck.

"This was my daughter's," Fuller said. "First wife. Gloria did it all up in pink and rag dolls; Raggedy Anns and Andys up the ass. I never liked 'em, their faces are like skulls. I liked 'em better after Dee-dee made a slingshot and took the head off every one. We swept up sawdust for a week. Had us a regular tomboy on our hands." His chuckle died out like a motor stalling. "After Gloria left and took her with her I put up all my school stuff and made it my thinking room. I thought my way through two more marriages out here."

"You must think on your feet." There wasn't any furniture.

"Everything's out on the grass. The rest goes next. I guess the feds will put the trophies and shit up on eBay and clean up. You'd be surprised how much some yutz will drop in his own home on something he wouldn't look twice at in a junk shop. You know, I had a chance to invest in Amazon at the start. They came to me. Know what I said? 'Bookstores don't make money.' "

"My old man told the same story about Xerox. He put his trust in carbon paper. *His* old man sold horse fodder across the street from the first Ford plant in Dearborn. I was born running out of the money."

Fuller wasn't listening. That part of the conversation had been over for a week. "I got your name from my ex-brother-in-law; third wife. He's with security at the library."

"Emory Freemantle. He lets me in the back door when they lock the front. A lot more detective work gets done at reading carrels than you see in the movies." I'd sprung Freemantle's nephew from a bum carjacking charge a couple of years ago.

"We still go to games. My track record with my in-laws is solid as hell." He planed a palm over the stubble on his head. The clump of gold and brilliants on his hand struck sparks in the sunlight coming through a window. "Dee-dee is Deirdre, all the flesh I've got. She turns twenty-five this year. When that happens she's got a trust fund coming to her in the amount of two million and change. The change being about what you'd need to live on for five years."

"You don't know that. Maybe I've got my own tax troubles."

"Such as what?"

"Such as I never make enough to owe any."

"Emory said you smart off too much, but I don't trust the big box agencies. My business manager had offices in America and Europe and wound up in Bimini. This is

14

her." He scooped a flat wallet out of a hip pocket, opened it, and handed me a snapshot. The girl had his gray eyes, but her coloring was lighter and her black hair was as straight as an Indian's. I seemed to remember his first wife was white. It wasn't as big a deal as it had been thirty years ago, but the outside pressure hadn't contributed to the relationship.

"She looks like a model," I said.

"I never could catch a break outside a stadium. Show me an ugly daughter and I'll show you a father who's at peace with the world." But his brief smile was more proud than bitter. "I can't touch the fund, thank God. I'd've sunk it in the restaurant chain and the car dealership and bribes to the Liquor Control Commission for the license I never got for the nightclub the city knocked down to put in another empty lot. That doesn't mean I'll stand around and watch her spend it on some puke who's no better than her old man."

I saw the job then. "This a specific puke, or a possible puke from the puke pool?"

"His name's Hilary Bairn." He spelled it, both names. "He says his family owns land in Scotland, but if they do it's on the bottom of Loch Ness. He and Dee-dee met at a college reunion in Ann Arbor. Only the

15

closest he ever got to attending Michigan was one semester at a community college in Ypsilanti. Business course. He's good about money, especially at knowing who's got it."

"It doesn't sound like I'm the first man on this detail."

"You can get almost anything off the Net. I don't know how a guy like you stays in business."

"You called me."

He set down his glass on a shelf, stood twisting his ring for ten seconds, then reached up to lift a trophy off a shelf higher up. I saw the year engraved in brass and a figure sprinting on top. Before the time of the designated hitter he'd come close to leading the American League in stolen bases. He used a pocketknife to unscrew a plate from the bottom and shook a thick roll of bills out into his palm. He replaced the trophy and held up the roll. The outside bill was a hundred.

"Fifty thousand," he said. "I squirreled it away where the bloodsuckers couldn't find it. You said on the phone you're bonded for up to a million?"

"The more I screw up, the more I'm worth. Only I've never screwed up that way. What makes you think Bairn will take it?"

He squinted at me as if I'd corked my bat.

"You're pretty quick."

I passed on that. "When does Deirdre turn twenty-five?"

"Two months."

"You don't have to be as good with money as you say Bairn is to know two months isn't too long to wait for two million. I've had my face laughed in before. You might not like it so much."

"I know some guys I can call if he does. You might let that slip when you're negotiating. I'd've called them first, only I'd rather be in debt to the government."

"He could pocket the cash and elope anyway. Then you'll have to call your guys and be into them and out fifty grand besides."

He took out his wallet again and handed me a folded square of paper. "You'll have him sign this agreement to stay away from Dee-dee before you give him the money. Then I'll show it to her. She won't believe me if it's just my word, but she's studying to pass the bar. A signature on a piece of paper means a lot more to her than her old dad's word. She'll do the rest."

I slid the snapshot inside the fold without opening it. "Is this about your daughter or the two million?"

"Yeah, you can ask that." But his face was

tight. "There's two times in your life when money doesn't mean anything: When you've got plenty and when you haven't got a cent. If I had it, I'd give it to him to get out of her life. I don't want her to make the same mistake her mother and the others did. Dee-dee's the only thing I ever did that counted. The rest is just a dusty column in *The Baseball Encyclopedia* and a cigar box full of trading cards."

A bawling, wordless voice drifted in from across the backyard and the other side of the big house, rising and falling like a wood chipper chewing up brush: The auctioneer had taken up his post and started his spiel. I asked Fuller what was stopping him from negotiating with Bairn himself.

"My face has been in the paper a lot more than yours. If it gets into the scandal sheets I've lost her forever. She'll take Bairn's side." He tossed the roll from one hand to the other and back. "You trying to talk yourself out of this job?"

"I just want to know what the job is. If you said rough him around and I said okay, he'd think he wandered into Baghdad, but I don't do that sort of work. I'll be your bag man, but I never split a knuckle on a jaw I didn't have personal issues with. I'm not one of those guys you can call."

18

"You don't have to worry about that. I don't send for a southpaw when a left-hander's at bat."

"I never really understood that."

"Me neither. If Sparky'd left me in in eighty-four the series would've been over in four. But you get what I mean."

I nodded. I'd heard all the sports metaphors I cared to for one day. "I charge a grand and a half up front. Got that much squirreled away besides the fifty?"

He slid the big ring off his finger and held it out. I took it. It was heavier than a .45 slug, solid gold or the next thing to it, with a diamond at each of the four points of a diamond shape on the dome. The engraving was worn, but still legible;

WORLD SERIES
1968

"Have it appraised," he said. "Take what the jeweler says and times it by ten. Don't hock it. I expect to buy it back when I scrape up the cash."

"Is it yours to give?"

The gray eyes turned to granite. "I didn't see any of them government suits in the outfield when I struck out Lou Brock."

Two

AMOS WALKER: Detective
HEIGHT: 6' 3/4"
WEIGHT: 185
SHOOTS: Right
BA: .199
HOME: Detroit, Michigan

That's how the trading card would read if they issued them for private investigators. Still a fair figure in the box, a little wind-worn, with silver tips in his five o'clock shadow. Strictly Flatbush, but when the windage is right and the sun's where it needs to be he can occasionally clear the fence in left field. And good job, because he runs bases like a three-legged dog. Anyway he hasn't been traded to Cleveland.

Hilary Bairn put his business degree to use keeping the books for a medical courier service in Mt. Clemens, a firm that sent frozen eyeballs to Australia and tongue depressers to Kansas City. The building was a Rubik's cube of aluminum and smoked glass across from St. Joseph's Mercy Hospital. At three minutes past five my first day at work he came off the elevator and went out across the baking sheet of a parking lot with me close on his heels. He had the lease on an orange Aztek, as ugly a piece of transportation as ever fell off the back of a haulaway. I'd gotten its registration from the secretary of state's office and was parked three slots down from it. I followed him into the street with my air conditioner wheezing a stench of scorched metal. I was in no hurry to make direct contact.

He was a handsome devil in a carefully dissipated sort of way, hair unbrushed and bleached corn yellow, a tiny loop in his left ear, and stubble on his cheeks and chin. They make razors now that crop off the top layer and leave the rest for seed. He was slender, not tall, in a cellophane-thin double-breasted that flapped unbuttoned when he walked, over a black T-shirt and a thin gold band around his neck. No one can do Euro trash as well as the Europeans, so the effect was slightly Halloweenish; when he parked in the narrow resident lot next to his apartment building and got out, a group of black youths waiting to cross the street swiveled their heads in his wake, smacking one another on the shoulder and grinning fit to split their heads in two. This was downtown, and the fashion cops had infiltrated the last sloppy ball cap and pair of baggy drawers. Bairn spun through the revolving door without appearing to notice.

I settled in to wait in a fifteen-minute zone across the street. Darius Fuller's fifty thousand and World Series ring sat in my bank box, a brisk walk from where I was staked out. The reason most private agents charge three days' pay in advance is it takes at least twenty-four hours to check the client's story. For all I knew the Hilary/Deirdre romance was a blind to cover the fact I was the mule in a drug deal or a contract killing.

So far everything checked out. Bairn lived straight up for a fish on the extreme right end of the food chain, but that's not so hard to do in a plastic society. The credit check I'd run said he'd missed two payments on the Aztek, had paid off his American Express bill on a Discover account, and spent next to nothing on the six hundred or so square feet he rented in a block of Woodward Avenue undergoing gentrification. Detroit had fallen off the list of the nation's ten most populous cities and landlords were waiving leases and damage deposits right and left just to make expenses. You could live like a king in the Motor City if you could put up with the meth lab in the palace down the hall.

The fifteen minutes ran out, and fifteen more, and no one rousted me. All four lanes filled with cars making the run home north to the developments and south to Jefferson and the Pointes. A mounted officer clip-clopped up the sidewalk looking for unbuckled seat belts and passed me right by. My guess was he wasn't going to discourage anyone who'd decided to stay put in town. I busied myself monkeying with the cellular telephone I'd bought to replace my electronic pager and the answering service I'd used for twenty-five years. The gizmo came with a forty-page manual translated by someone who'd learned his Japanese in a Greek restaurant and his English in Mexico City. Its nearest relay tower was assembly-required; it stopped sending and receiving signals every time its aircraft light went off and on. I had a two-year service contract.

After forty minutes all the air had begun to rush out of rush hour, and Hilary Bairn came out of the building jiggling his keys. He'd ditched the suit and put on a pair of pressed cargo pants and those running shoes that wink at you from the heels. When the Aztek nosed out into the uptown lane I turned over the engine and fell in two cars behind.

Entering westbound I-96 we nudged our way through a knot that had tied itself to observe a motorist changing a tire on the right shoulder and lockstepped through eight miles of barrels and barricades and no construction going on. West of Dearborn Heights we opened up to eighty-five, passing a few and getting passed by a lot. I hung back between eight and twelve car lengths, changing lanes only when it became necessary to avoid crawling up the trunk of a daisy-picker doing seventy. So far as I could tell, Bairn never looked up into his rearview mirror. We swirled down a ramp that turned into a complete circle, coasted into the town of Plymouth, and crept along streets made into tunnels by shade trees past gift and antiques shops and strollers in flip-flops and shorts. It's a painted-tin community, strictly for the amusement of transients and for commuters from Detroit and the college towns to the west to lay their heads.

Finally he turned into a square lot next to the Mayflower Hotel, a convincing example of Tudor architecture near the main four corners, and slid into the last slot. I drove around the block and found a spot next to the curb. All the meters had been pulled up by the roots years before to encourage trade. Inside, the chief attraction was the restaurant, cool and timbered and paneled with piano music treacling from the direction of the bar. Bairn was seated in a booth at the back, chatting with a waitress filling his water glass from a pitcher. I went to the bar, took a stool, and asked the chunky party who came up to me for a Corona.

"Lime?"

"No, I'm watching my weight."

He forged a die-cast bartender's smile and clunked down a bottle and a glass on a square napkin. Smoke curled from the neck and beads glistened like freshwater pearls on the outside of the bottle. I let the glass stand and drank directly from the source. The cold seared my teeth.

A few minutes later Deirdre Fuller came in, paused to let her eyes catch up with the light, then smiled and walked Bairn's way. She wore her straight black hair in a diagonal across her forehead, bending out just below the ears, and a white summer dress that clung to all the hollows and drifted around her knees. Her shoulders and arms and legs were bare, her feet bare in white cork sandals, an even caramel in contrast. She was a living hot-fudge sundae.

Bairn smiled up from his seat, didn't rise when she slid in opposite him, and when the waitress returned ordered for himself first. That buried whatever sympathy I might have had for Hilary Bairn. I nursed my beer while they ate and conversed in low voices lost in the rustle as others came in to dine. When the bartender asked if I wanted another I started to shake my head, then caught the movement out of the tail of my eye when Bairn leaned over to take something from a pocket in his cargo pants. I nodded and pushed aside the first bottle, which had grown tepid.

The something was a small humpbacked box. I seemed to have happened upon a momentous occasion. But the box was too big for an occasion that large.

He let her open it. It contained a gold watch with a blue dial and a link band, too heavy for the feminine wrist. She snapped the lid shut without comment and slid it into her purse, woven white leather with a rolled handle. The meal finished in silence. When the check came, he paid for it with a card, got up finally to kiss her, signed the receipt, and went out past the bar with her on his arm. A light scent of sweet almonds came behind her.

I paid for the beers and stood outside the entrance from the parking lot tapping a cigarette on the back of the pack as Bairn and Deirdre separated, he to the left, she to the right, toward an emerald Mini Cooper with a white convertible top. I made up my mind to let Bairn go, trotted to my car, and followed the smaller vehicle. That watch had me curious. Several blocks ahead, Bairn's Aztek turned onto the expressway headed home, but Deirdre continued past and swung south on Beck Road. Her father had said she clerked in a law office in Westland but kept an apartment in Ann Arbor, where she'd entered the law program at the University of Michigan last fall. She took I-94 west in that direction. She exited in Ypsilanti.

In Depot Town, a Bohemian neighborhood of pubs and curiosity shops that had sprung up around the old train station, we parked on gravel and I watched her trot around the corner of a pawnshop. I had my hand on the door handle to follow her on foot when she turned in at the pawnshop door. I settled back and cracked a window to smoke.

Just as I poked the stub out through the crack she came back out, cork heels clocking, both hands on the purse held in front of her and a pinched look on her face. She underhanded the purse into the Mini Cooper's passenger seat, got in, ground the starter, and sprayed gravel backing around and powering out into the street. The driver of a light pickup chirped his brakes to avoid getting clipped and made a mincing little noise with his horn.

I didn't follow Deirdre. Instead I got out and went into the pawnshop. A buzzer sounded when I opened the door. There were bars on the windows and the counter had a steel cage on top with a gate that slid to one side to allow the free exchange of goods and currency. You can tell a lot about an enterprise from its fixtures. This one was tricked out like Jackson State Prison.

The man behind the counter was a young Arab with a blue chin. I didn't mess around with a story or the honorary sheriff's badge. Pawnshop clerks have heard them all and seen every star and shield. I poked a twenty-dollar bill through the cage. He didn't look at it, only at me. His face assumed a patience of biblical proportions.

"A light-skinned black woman was just in," I said. "Buy anything from her?"

"No." He snatched the bill from between my fingers before I could exert counterpressure. From there on in it was up to my personal charm — and whatever else I had in my wallet.

"Why not?"

He said nothing.

I blew out air. "You guys. Why do you have to make it a chore? A couple of bars doesn't make you a hard guy. A monkey's got those."

He reached under the counter and clonked a Glock on top. It had a brushed-metal finish and black composition grips.

I showed him my ID. "I'm working for her father. Darius Fuller, maybe you know the name. Follow sports?"

His face changed then. You could have knocked me over with a mortar. It was like watching the toughest head on Rushmore crack a grin.

"I was in the bleachers when he threw the no-hitter," he said. "No joke, that was the Fuller Brush Man's little girl?"

"If you'd bought the watch you'd have a souvenir."

The face shut back down. "The price tag was still in the box. Whoever lifted it was too dumb to tear it in half."

I put away the ID folder. "Thanks, brother."

"Famous men's kids. You know?"

"She wasn't the one who lifted it. If it makes any difference."

He thought about that. "It checks. She seemed madder about it than I was."

"Report it?"

"To who, the police? I reported every funny customer I'd be on the phone all day. I'd report you," he said.

I thanked him again and left.

I drove back to Detroit, stopped in the office to pay some bills and study the cell phone manual again under a bright light, decided that knowing how to retrieve messages wasn't a high priority in the current business climate, and went home to a sandwich, a drink, two hours of police drama and funny home videos of cats on fire, and bed.

Sleep took its time coming. The Fourth of July was still days off, but that didn't keep some of the neighbors from test-firing the ordnance they'd smuggled in from roadside stands in Indiana: There were thumps, stuttering strings of firecrackers, and now and then the bass note of a shotgun. I lit a cigarette without turning on the light and blew smoke at a ceiling that glimmered from time to time in the reflective burst of a bottle rocket, wondering if all those stories I'd read and movies I'd seen about misunderstood suitors were full of hooey. The worst part of the work is on some level you always hope the client is wrong.

Next day I did all the morning stuff, put on my second-best suit, and took my spot in the loading zone across from Hilary Bairn's apartment house just in time to watch him leave for the office in Mt. Clemens. Then I rode up to his floor in a brass Otis on a smooth new cable and let myself into his apartment with my nifty pocket burglar kit. I wasted time on Bairn's underwear drawer and medicine cabinet and porno library, then looked at his appointment calendar, fixed with a magnetic strip to the refrigerator in the toy kitchen. He'd drawn a line through his most recent appointment, the day before yesterday:

2:00 p.m. Sing

Nothing in Bairn's profile had indicated any particular interest in music; but in the circles I turned in, *Sing* meant something else.

THREE

Most Detroiters have never heard of Detroit Beach, a quiet little sun-faded community where gulls and sun-worshippers go to avoid the crowds on Belle Isle and at Port Huron. Few of them know they owe the spot to the pioneers who chopped down trees four generations ago to land high-powered boats loaded to the gunnels with whiskey smuggled from Canada; by then the Detroit riverfront was filled with U.S. Coast Guardsmen with their hands out, and nearby Monroe with rival machine-gunners. The balmy days of Michigan are few, and bright umbrellas tend to sprout on every bloody patch of shore.

In summer it's a good place to go to watch girls in cutoffs and bandanna blouses riding skiffs and old men with faces heavy with time fishing for walleye. The big auto and tech money is five hours north on the Michigan Riviera, polishing the brass on their boats in Grand Traverse Bay and taking horseback riding lessons on Mackinac Island. But today the never-idle rich were missing a bet. The weatherwonks were reporting thunderstorms up there while Lake Huron was sliding into Detroit Beach in long creamy swells like poured pudding. I parked in a public area and went down to the water first, taking off my coat and walking along the damp stain left by the tide with the coat over one shoulder, smoking and feeling my sodden shirt separate itself in patches from my back in the breeze across the bay. The mist felt like a veil of cool silk on my face.

A tatty little arcade just up from the beach sold ice cream and tackle, and behind it stood a blue-and-white-striped pavilion designed to look like a Hollywood version of a sultan's tent. In the days of the big bands it had sheltered a ballroom, and for a little while a roller-skating rink. A snap-letter sign stuck in a swatch of grass identified it now as a community recreation center, where seniors played bridge and bingo and youths shot pool. That was the chamber of commerce's interpretation. Natives and the grapevine along the I-75 corridor knew it as a place to bet on sports and the turn of the wheel without having to share one's winnings with Lansing and Washington. The legislators who swung the vote for legal casinos and the state lottery said such places were obsolete, but they failed to count on the universal American faith in the left-handed dollar.

I climbed a rickrack set of steps angling steeply up from the beach and followed the decking around to the entrance, which fronted on the Dixie Highway. Cars were parked on the broken asphalt set aside for them, and on the edge under shade trees a double-bottom tractor-trailer rig idled, as long as the arcade. Out on the highway apron a pair of gulls squared off over a greasy Taco Bell sack, fluttering at each other and falling back to regroup. I flicked my cigarette butt their way, just to see if it would change the dynamic. A bird hopped over to investigate, pecked at the butt, and returned to the field of battle just in time to prevent the other gull from taking off with the sack. They fought, squawking like rusty car doors, and then things were back where they'd started. It was an *Animal Planet* moment.

I didn't have to contend with a peephole panel or a bouncer at the door; I barely had to contend with a door. It stood half open, blocked by a homemade boat anchor fashioned from an iron ring sunk in a paint bucket filled with cement. Famously, the pavilion wasn't air-conditioned, like Wrigley Field before they installed lights. The dealers and customers counted for ventilation on the crossdraft between highway and lake, where glass doorwalls opened on screens looking out on the beach. Air circulated, as a matter of fact, but it smelled of crapshooters' armpits and the sour pulp of mildew from the green baize on the game tables.

A sign at the door prohibited bare feet and swimsuits, but apart from that the dress code was casual, shorts and sandals. They went like hell with the Japanese lanterns and pastel murals of peacocks and cherry blossoms. The age of the players gathered at the rails and perched in front of the slots ranged from First Communion to Last Rites. An eighty-year-old woman in a red wig and a blue sundress gave a cigarette cough of a laugh when her dealer dealt her blackjack; a boy of fourteen in a black T-shirt that hung to his knees cursed and struck a one-armed bandit with the flat of his hand. The house men and women were almost exclusively Asian; illegal enterprises almost never feel compelled to conform to equal opportunity employment. Wild hair and piercings seemed to be banned, but Hawaiian shirts and short skirts were okay, depending on the amount of growth on the chest and the girth of the thighs. It was a resort place, they didn't want to scare off customers sticky from the beach. The slots and poker machines chimed and cackled and played Bach's "Toccata and Fugue in D Minor" on the organ, *Phantom of the Opera* style; Disneyland for the decadent middle class.

The pit boss by the roulette wheel was dressed to blend in with the customers, but they all run to 46 portly and haven't a live nerve in their faces. I beckoned him over. He glided on rubber heels with his fingers curled under at his hips.

"Boss lady in?" I asked.

He had the face of a sumo wrestler, all ovals stacked one atop another, squashing his eyes nearly shut and his lips as tight as sliced bacon. He inserted his tongue between them to let words out. "Who's that?"

"Mrs. Sing. The name on the bail ticket every time the cops push the place in."

He said nothing for a glacial age, and when I remembered I had a summer tax bill due in September I foraged in the coat over my forearm and held out a card. "Give this to whoever's watching the register."

The wheel paid out twice, then one of the hands rose and I stuck the card between two stubby fingers. He turned and left, moving steadily and without haste, but making time. Once you get a boulder going there's very little that can slow it down.

While I waited a couple of slots paid off, not big, and a pretty Asian waitress in wedge-heeled sandals with long muscles in her thighs came over and offered me a drink from a tray. I shook my head and poked a dollar under a tall glass of bourbon with a cube floating in it for garnish. Two of those and you lost track of where you'd parked the car, not to mention the odds and percentages. She smiled and prowled away.

"Mr. Walker? I'm Victor Cho. I own this establishment."

He'd appeared at my elbow, coming up more quietly than the sumo: a slender Korean of sixty or so wearing a blue silk sport shirt, gray gabardine slacks, and glistening loafers with hard toes. He had a horseshoe of receding black hair and a polite smile that showed his eyeteeth.

The hard toes were the clue. There would be no stomping on them and taking him off guard. The big man with the wrestler's face stood behind him, as distant and as close as Mt. Fuji.

"How do you do," I said. "Actually, my business is with Mrs. Sing."

"I don't know anyone of that name in this country. Do you have a complaint?"

"I seem to have lost Mrs. Sing."

"Someone is kidding you. Eliot will see you to your car."

"Eliot?"

Mt. Fuji shifted its weight onto the balls of his feet.

As Mr. Cho turned to take himself out of the line of charge, I touched his wrist. "Eliot can probably take me," I said. "He knows all the steps and I'm rusty. I left the sawed-off home. But we'll bust up furniture, and you know how sound travels on the water. There's always one cop who's just looking for an excuse to bust up the rest, and at the height of tourist season."

He brushed off my hand with a little movement. "Believe me, I'd like to help you out. I don't know any Madame Sing."

"Who said 'Madame?' "

His expression changed then. The smile hadn't let up even when I'd offered to renovate the place with Eliot. Now he looked solemn. "Madame Sing owns the property this pavilion stands on. My only contact with her is when I send the rent check to her post office box in Detroit. She has nothing to do with this business."

"I didn't say she did."

38

He held up my card as if reading it for the first time. "You're available at this number?"

"Not all the time." I plucked it out of his hand, unclipped the pen from inside my coat, and wrote the cell phone number on the back. I returned the card. "That one's good when it's working. Tell her to keep trying."

"Does she need to know what it's about?"

"Hilary Bairn."

"Who's he?"

It was my turn to show my eyeteeth. "Strike two, Victor. Most people would've asked, 'Who's she?'"

He looked at me, but there wasn't any satisfaction in it. It was like firing a shot into quicksand.

Heading back north I hit heavy traffic, with ribbons of heat rising as thick as blown glass from radiators and the back of drivers' necks, but the trip hadn't been wasted. I'd have been disappointed if Madame Sing were as easy to see as the bay.

Charlotte Sing was an Amerasian, a refugee of the Korean Police Action brought to the U.S. through a sea of red tape by her father, an American serviceman who'd spent five years after the cease-fire looking for her after her mother died in an internment camp in Pyongyang; somesuch place like that, that sounded like a rubber band breaking. Legend said the father had wanted only an unpaid housemaid, and used his belt when the service was unsatisfactory. At age sixteen, Charlotte's petition for emancipation had been granted and she'd gone to work for one of the Oriental massage parlors proliferating throughout the Detroit area.

Ordinarily her story would have ended there, and not with musical accompaniment. It was a yellow-slave racket, where truckers went to get their gears shifted by young women who'd been taken off their parents' hands in Korea by sponsors who let them work off their debt as prostitutes. Most of the girls wound up in jail or dead of disease, but Charlotte was smarter than most, and turned what she'd learned inward. She married one of the sponsors, put her clothes back on, and took over the bookkeeping. When the law caught up with Andrew Sing, she'd taken the stand against him. She forgot her English when the defense tried to cross-examine. Sing was convicted.

The proceeds of his enterprises never surfaced. It was determined he'd reinvested everything and lost it all when the law cracked down. But two years after his appeals ran out and he began serving thirty years in the federal correctional institution in Milan, Michigan, Charlotte began buying up choice plots of real estate across the Great Lakes region, where in the course of time casinos and health spas and after-hours bars opened up, always illegal, but with no paper trail connecting the landlady to the businesses themselves. There's no law against owning rental property where the tenants break the law. She charged astronomically high rents — according to the books she kept in her own hand — but none of her customers complained. In this way she managed to make millions off gambling and prostitution and declare every dollar on her Form 1040 without interference either from local authority or the departments of Treasury and Justice.

She lived in seclusion, it was said, dividing her time among her homes on Lake Michigan, in Bloomfield Hills, and north of San Francisco, and an office on Detroit's West Side in a polyglot neighborhood populated mostly by Vietnamese, Japanese, and Korean immigrants and their children. No driver's license was on record in her name and her passport photo was generic Asian, ordinary almost to the point of invisibility. For drama, the press fell back on a forty-year-old image of a scrawny sixteen-year-old challenging her father's custody in court.

The press didn't take interest in her often; it had enough headline-happy multimillionaires to go around. But that was changing.

When a state attorney general who wanted to be governor tried to subpoena her to appear before a grand jury investigating vice, she'd hired two Asian women of her approximate age and build to accompany her everywhere she went, in outfits identical to hers. With no reliable photo and only a description to go by, the servers were at a loss to know whom to approach. "Well, we all look alike," was her only comment when a writer for the *Metro Times* got a call through to her office. The jury's term ran out and she returned to California and her army of realtors.

The device backfired. That human shell game was clever stage business, but it and her flip rejoinder were too colorful for the peace of mind of a woman who set a premium on privacy. Overnight she went from an object of vague curiosity to a celebrity, and a sinister one at that: a creature between Greta Garbo and Heidi Fleiss. Even her name and exotic title sounded like something out of a pulp magazine from the days of the Yellow Peril. When a bartender at the Union Street Saloon on Woodward assembled a drink from green tea and gin and christened it a "Madame Sling," the patrons streamed in for a sample. Within a week, the establishment received a letter produced on expensive stationery, signed by a former justice of the Michigan State Supreme Court, demanding the name of the drink be changed. The bar complied and the customer flow ebbed to normal, but by then that old photograph of a teenage Charlotte had resurfaced and appeared in newspapers and over the shoulders of TV anchors across the country.

Charlotte Sing was one of the twenty wealthiest women in America, according to *Forbes* and *Fortune.* According to the calendar in Hilary Bairn's apartment, he'd had an appointment with her the day before yesterday. Whatever a fortune-hunting petty thief with a bad bleach job had to talk about with the Queen of Vice, I doubted it was the double-entry system of bookkeeping.

FOUR

Just as the caged city overpasses began to close over my head, my cell went off for the first time. The musicians on the NPR station I listened to for jazz were teaching themselves something progressive, and for a moment I thought the tone was part of the melody. When it continued into the deejay's commentary, I unholstered the instrument and said "Hello" into a dead signal. A moment later I got a different sort of ring that I figured out meant I had a message. Nothing I tried could retrieve it and I'd left the manual at the office. There, the telephone on the desk was ringing.

"I left word on your walkabout," Darius Fuller said. "I had an easier time getting the general manager on the phone when I couldn't put one over the plate in three games."

I sat down in the swivel. "I said I had one. I didn't say I knew how to use it. What's the emergency?"

"That's the word. Your two months just became two days. I had a fight with Dee-dee this morning, about you know who. She got mad and said she's going to elope."

"You hired me to handle it. I ought to charge you extra for helping, the way plumbers do."

"This a joke to you? You got a kid?"

"No, I've been a detective all my life. Why two days? You can buy a ladder at Home Depot any time."

"She's got an oral exam tomorrow. I guess I should be happy she isn't planning to give up the law and start shelling out little Dee-dees and Hilaries. I don't feel happy."

"Maybe that's the point. She's just trying to make you madder than you were already. She didn't look any too pleased with her future intended when I saw her last night."

"I'm paying you to see Bairn."

"If they weren't sometimes a package deal, you wouldn't be paying me at all. I'll tell you all about it when we meet. Bairn's got problems. If they're as bad as they're starting to look, we might get him at your price."

A rattling breath drew on his end. "You could be right, it could be a balk. A bluff. I can't risk it. If they make it legal, that trust fund's as good as in his pocket. I didn't work my way out of the minors and get arterioscopic surgery twice to see her piss it all away on a foul ball like him."

"There's also your daughter's happiness."

"According to her mother, I bobbled that one a long time back. But I never heard Dee-dee complain until this morning. She asked me what right I had to give her advice on her life when I wasn't around for most of it."

"Those away games are hell on family."

"Just between you and me and whoever's eavesdropping on the line, it wasn't just the away games. There's a lot of temptation hangs around the locker room after a win. You got to have iron to resist. I used up all mine in the infield."

"Tell her that?"

"I figured she had it from her mother. You going to brace Bairn?"

"I won't stop for coffee. With two months to payoff, he's taking risks he might not if he knows he can seal the deal with your daughter this week. If she's bluffing, or if he hasn't heard from her since before you two blew up, I might get him to take less than what you're willing to put on the table. Otherwise —"

"You don't need to waste time spelling it out. Get going and steal second." The connection broke.

I called Bairn's line at the courier service in Mt. Clemens. It was a half hour until quitting, and if he hadn't heard from Deirdre, I needed to get him away before he did.

The office voice mail kicked in after four rings. I went to the switchboard, got patched through to someone in his department, and found out he'd left early. That was a bad sign. He might be having an early dinner with his fiancée.

He didn't answer his cell either. I clicked off at the beginning of a generic outgoing announcement and tried him at home. Someone picked up.

"Hello?"

I hadn't heard him speak all the time I'd been following him. It was a tired sort of voice, not at all the tone of a man about to inherit a wife and a fortune. I took that as a good sign. Maybe she hadn't told him the news, or maybe she'd been bluffing after all when she'd told her father.

"Hilary Bairn?"

"Yes?"

I told him my name and occupation. "The party I represent wishes to propose an arrangement that will benefit you financially and immediately. I'd like to discuss it with you in person as soon as possible."

"How much is the benefit?"

"It's substantial." I clamped my mouth shut on the end of it. I couldn't have made it sound more final if I'd popped a cheek with my finger.

"You know my address?"

I recited it. "I can be there in ten minutes."

"Okay, Walker."

I hung up on the dial tone and went to the bank.

A FedEx truck had the loading zone across from Bairn's apartment nailed down. I dipped into equity for a spot in a lot around the corner on Lafayette and strode back, racing against time and Deirdre Fuller; the fact that Bairn was even in a mood to discuss money gave me hope and anxiety in equal doses.

The building had been a department store back when Detroit had them, with an iron front and three floors above the two-story ground floor where the money was counted and inventory recorded and for the general manager to tilt back and blow wreaths of blue cigar smoke from behind a desk the size of an emerging African nation. There was still a depression in the elevator floor near the push buttons where an operator had sat on a stool to work the lever. Old wood continued its aromatic deterioration under the new drywall and paint. I knocked on Bairn's door, got no answer, and tried the knob just for the hell of it. I'd left the burglar kit at home. It makes a bad impression to jimmy your way in to a friendly business conference.

The knob turned without resistance. I took my hand off it and knocked again.

Nothing. I put my ear to the door, but they hadn't replaced it with a modern hollow-core and it was like trying to listen for signs of activity from outside a bank vault.

For once in my life I went with my first instinct and walked away from an unlocked door. Unlocked doors are no good, not in a city where kids chain their skateboards to parking meters. There, only two kinds of people don't lock up when they're expecting a stranger, and Hilary Bairn wasn't a tourist. I'd had plenty enough of the other kind to kill my curiosity.

I didn't make it back to the elevator, of course. The cops had set their trap from behind another door across the hall and came out with guns drawn.

FIVE

The cop who'd pretended to be Bairn when I'd called was a large black detective third-grade named Burrough, no s, fifty and natty as Easter Sunday in a spotless white Panama and tan Palm Beach suit, gusseted to accommodate the harness. I think he'd transferred from the mayor's security detail after a dustup of some kind with a reporter from Channel 7. I'd seen Burrough around headquarters once or twice and he'd seemed jolly, but then I'd had a pass to the fourth floor and no manacles on my wrists. I didn't have them on now, but I got the impression there were orders pending on that.

He sat me down at the table in Bairn's kitchen and went through my personal items: a wallet containing a ten and two singles, an empty Winstons pack, fourteen scattered cents, a set of keys, a cell phone in its spring clip, and my ID folder with the toy badge. I'd left the registered Chief's

Special in the safe in my office and extra-legal Luger in the car. I hadn't come in prepared to shoot off any locks. Altogether it didn't take up much space and looked kind of sad for a man on the thready outer edge of middle age.

Oh, and fifty thousand in cash in a Number Ten envelope. I kept forgetting about that.

He counted the bills, using the eraser end of a mechanical pencil to fan them out and then nudge them back inside the envelope. The FBI was watching the department that year and I guessed he didn't want to take the chance of anything sticking in the heat.

"Sell short?" That same tired voice I'd heard on the telephone.

I said nothing.

"Standing mute?"

"Conserving energy," I said. "It's hot. Guns drawn means I'd have to tell it all over again to a lieutenant or better. It's that kind of case."

"Know the system, do you?"

"I've got cable."

"You're not under arrest. Just detained. So far there's no law against knocking on a door, even —" He checked himself. "I could be out of date on that. The mail from Washington's slow this time of year."

"I tried the knob, too, don't forget."

One of the uniforms tagged in, a long-jawed officer built like a marionette, loose in the joints, with the eyes of a born bully. He'd popped a couple of seams checking me for weapons. "Let's house him, Detective. He's long on smart answers and short on cooperation."

"I wish you'd rush it through," I said. "Tonight's corned beef at County."

Burrough got a dreamy look and slapped me.

He'd pulled it, but he had a hand like a sap glove, heavy and hard, and I almost lost my seat. I felt a palm-shaped welt rising on my cheek, but I didn't touch it. This was a variation on an old game: bad cop, bad cop. It told me everything I needed to know about what was in the part of Bairn's apartment I hadn't seen yet that afternoon. I'd had a pretty good idea anyway, from the level of tension in the room.

"You should file a complaint for that," he said in the tired voice that came from asking questions he didn't believe the answers to. "Our new lady chief wants a twenty-first-century department, all sharp creases and no blood on the blouse."

"Women," I said.

"Too much pressure. From the walking

scrotums on the street and the brass hats downtown and the cockroaches with briefcases and the assholes from the press and now the Fucking Bureau of Infestation. Enough people tell you you're shit you start to stink."

I touched the welt then, to cover the surprise. It was an apology of sorts, and an apology from a cop is rare and a little pathetic, like watching an old lifeguard let out his belly when he thinks no one can see.

"I asked for it," I said, "though I thought it would come from Gumby here. Not bad at all, and without even a running start."

"Thanks. These kids huff and puff and waste too much time. You got to be quick if you don't want to get caught on video."

We were friends again.

"Who the fuck's Gumby?" said the officer.

His partner, a solid Mexican whose eyebrows and moustache made parallel bars across his pie-tin face, came in from the living room. At one time or another they'd all gone in there, leaving someone behind to watch me, to return seconds later with no expression. I figured that's where the attraction was.

"Shift change in ten minutes," the Mexican told Burrough. "When's the inspector coming?"

"When he comes. Got a roast in the oven?"

"Well, I got a life, same as everybody."

"Speak for yourself."

"Inspector," I said.

The brim of the Panama came up. "You say something?"

"I wouldn't think a downtown stiff rated."

Burrough jumped on it. "Who said anything about a stiff?"

"Okay, 'horizontal American.' "

There was a little silence after that. Nothing pregnant; the cast had simply gone up on the script.

The shift ran out. I heard it in the sudden quiet from the main drag when the escape traffic stopped in midsurge and the people who were stuck in town — stuck because they lived there — popped open the first can of apres-ski Stroh's and plunked down in Naugahyde waiting for the microwave to beep. Detective Burrough jingled the keys and change in his pocket, the Mexican pursed his lips in a dry whistle, Gumby standing behind me shifted his weight from one noisy new oxford to the other. The grapes of wrath grew heavy on the vine.

The hall door opened and shut and then John Alderdyce, inspector in charge of

Homicide, slid in like a lake freighter from the little breezeway that separated the kitchen from the living room where the dead slumbered; or so I thought, and my confirmation had just arrived. The tidy bachelor's kitchen was packed to capacity now.

I hadn't seen John in months. If he'd changed at all it was in the direction he'd been going since puberty, bigger and harder and dressed more carefully than the governor, in wine-colored summer worsted with spectators on his feet and a gray silk figured tie on a shirt of the same shade. His face was made from scrap iron and bitumen, black and angular, and the whites of his eyes burned like hearts of fire deep in their sockets. They went from Gumby to the Mexican and finally to Burrough. To him I was dust in a corner. He was as good a friend as I had.

"Press?" he asked.

"Not yet," said the detective. "It went out as a disturbance complaint. I talked to the neighbor. Got it when you need it." He patted the breast pocket of his Palm Beach suit. Next to Alderdyce's it looked like molded plastic.

"Show me."

Burrough gave the uniforms the stay-put

look and led the way out of the kitchen.

They were gone five minutes. The Mexican checked his watch six times and Gumby redistributed his weight twice, creaking like a gallows. The building shuddered when the elevator trundled up and down the shaft. Bairn's neighbors were coming home, changing clothes, and going back out to try their luck at the MGM Grand and Motor City casinos and the Indian trap in Greektown.

I had a sudden thought and looked at the refrigerator. The thickset uniform saw the movement. He was twice the cop his partner was, but he'd probably finish out his service in the blue bag, because everyone knew Mexicans are hardworking and as slow as the tide. I turned it into a full rotation, as if I had a stiff neck, and went back to counting the specks on the tabletop. I'd seen what I'd expected to.

Alderdyce and Burrough came back and the inspector scraped back a chair and sat down across from me and slid aside my effects to lay his forearms on the table. He looked at me then for the first time, but spoke to the detective. "Who hit him?"

"Me, Inspector. He was being an asshole and I didn't want Officer Ransom to get himself in trouble."

So Gumby's name was Ransom. I thought I might need it if the feds recommended a clean sweep at the top and he got promoted.

"Break his nose next time. He won't file."

"Hello to you, too, John," I said. "Can I bum a cigarette?"

"Those things'll take ten years off your life."

"Just the lousy ones at the end."

"Try the patch?"

I shook my head. "Couldn't keep it lit."

"You see, Inspector?" said Ransom.

"I've seen." To me: "Well, I finished quitting, so you can tell your lungs to hold their water. Who's paying?"

"Nobody. I came to see a friend."

"You told Burrough on the phone you represented someone with a proposition."

"The proposition was a beer, and the someone was Anheuser-Busch. We joke like that all the time."

"You're usually funnier than that."

"Thanks. I never thought you were listening."

"What's the name on the lease?" he asked Burrough without lifting his eyes from mine.

"Hilary Bairn."

"Where'd you two meet?" he asked me.

"Some bar."

He twitched a little finger wearing his

University of Detroit class ring; all the others had grown too thick to fit. "You need to be careful where you go in this town with that much cash on you."

"I figure I'm in the same boat with it or without it."

"It's your money?"

"It's my pocket."

"We're supposed to report this kind of thing to the IRS. It could put you in a higher tax bracket."

"I'd like to be in a bracket. Last year I didn't even file a return."

Ransom said, "I was telling Detective Burrough we should house him, Inspector. Obstruction of justice."

I decided to get mad. "I made a telephone call and knocked on a door. Next thing I know I'm getting hosed down, slapped, and held without benefit of tobacco. I'm the one being obstructed."

Alderdyce didn't stir a molecule. "Feel better?"

"A little. I could use that smoke."

"It isn't what you did," he said. "It's the number you called and the door you knocked on and the day you picked to do it."

"How was he killed?"

Nothing. He'd built the wall over more

than thirty years of interrogating suspects in rooms like that one and downtown and being interrogated by defense lawyers in the Frank Murphy Hall of Justice. I said, "It's homicide because that's your detail. I'm having trouble getting from there to why a bookkeeper in Mt. Clemens draws a visit from the top brass in Detroit. Where's Mary Ann?"

"Lieutenant Thaler's interviewing in Washington. Going to be a lady U.S. marshal."

"Sorry to hear it."

"I didn't know you had a case against her."

"I don't. I'll miss her. All four of you guys are cute as shovels. I was looking forward to the treat."

"She won't get the job," he said. "The politicians make a lot of noise about equal opportunity, but it's the bureaucrats who do the hiring. They'll take one look at those big brown eyes and tell her her app's on file."

"Not if they take a look at her folder."

"They'll say it was sweetened. The chief's a woman."

"Bet you twenty she gets the job."

"Kind of lean, with fifty grand at your fingertips."

"I didn't save it up being careless."

"You going to keep running with that?"

"Until I get tired."

One of his big shoulders moved. It was like watching a water buffalo adjusting its load. "Always happy to take your money. Care to see the damage?"

"I might as well. He didn't pick these chairs for comfort."

"Showing our age, are we?"

"Doing our best not to." I got up, using my good leg for leverage. He rose smoothly and all of a piece. We'd been poking nails into each other like that since we were calves.

A red-and-black wool rug covered the living room floor to within eighteen inches of the walls, exposing the original hardwood, two-inch strips sanded and stained golden brown and sealed with poly. The walls were eggshell, with mall prints in frames of giraffes and gourds and construction workers eating lunch on a girder twenty stories above the street. I couldn't see a theme. The furniture was Pottery Barn, with wormholes drilled into it. Bairn had dropped more money he didn't have on a liquid-crystal TV on a metal stand with drawers to hold the VCR and DVD player and a small collection of movies and CDs. I didn't like the place any more than I had that morning, and the fact that someone had kicked over a lamp and a potted plant and knocked a picture off plumb was no improvement. The body on the floor wasn't even Hilary Bairn's.

Six

Alderdyce put on a pair of disposable latex gloves from his pocket, bent, and lifted the woman's head from the floor to give me a better look at the face. She lay in a loose braid, on her back with her hips twisted sideways and her head turned so only her profile showed when you were standing over her. She'd exchanged the white summer dress for a yellow linen jacket and slacks and a knit black top. One of her open-toed pumps, black patent leather, was off her bare foot. Her flap of black hair fell down over one eye when her head was lifted. The other eye was looking at something way outside my range.

"We never met," I said.

"Deirdre Jacqueline Fuller." Detective Burrough read from a spiral pad. "Name on her driver's license, and the photo checked. She had a key in her purse that fit the apartment door." He tilted his Panama toward a shiny black handbag on an end table.

Alderdyce lowered her head to the rug. The puddle of drool had begun to dry. "Lab monkeys won't thank you for laying on hands," Burrough said.

"What they going to do, stomp my toes in their paper shoes?"

"They were okay before. It was that TV show turned them into arrogant pricks."

"Head trauma?" Alderdyce asked.

"Bruise on the left temple. I make it she fell and hit the floor lamp on the corner of the metal shade. Or somebody pushed her."

"Accident?"

"I don't see how you could plan it. You can land punches on the temple all day and miss the sweet spot."

"Well, maybe we won't have it long. Five hundred hours community service and three years probation if he cops. Anyone see Bairn?"

"Neighbor heard the door slam after the commotion in the living room. He didn't look out. Didn't hear the elevator, so he figured whoever it was took the stairs. Stewed for a little and then called it in. Ransom and Ordoñez caught the squeal. They found the door unlocked and called me when they saw this.

"Be different it was a couple blocks

north," he went on. "Voices raised, slap on the chops, that's a day in the life. Down here they're interested in stopping things before they slide back."

Alderdyce stripped off the gloves, watching me. "How long since you went to a Tigers game?"

"When did they close down the stadium?" I asked.

"It's the same team, no matter where they play."

"Same jerseys. Different names on the back. I lost touch. You trying to get rid of an extra ticket?"

"It wasn't a social question. You really don't know who Deirdre Fuller is."

"Another friend of Bairn's, apparently."

"Her father's Darius Fuller: the Fuller Brush Man. That's how come she rates an inspector. The mayor takes it hard when the children of famous locals come to bad ends. Especially when it's inside city limits. In a couple of hours this place is going to be crawling with media."

"Assholes." Burrough swept shut his notepad.

"The detective's beef is personal. Mine's professional. When they stick their corn dogs in my face and start yapping questions, it would be nice to say we're questioning her boyfriend. It's always the boyfriend, so they'll accept that and stand back and give us some air. If you did know Bairn casually, you should be able to shed some light on their relationship, what it was and if they got along, but you say you didn't know her. If, and I know it goddamn well to be true, he's business, you do know. So is he the client or the subject of the investigation?"

"He isn't a client."

"Progress. Who's the payroll?"

"I didn't say there was one."

"Bullshit. You made a business call to this number and you didn't even know it wasn't Bairn's voice on the line. The only way you'd make that mistake is if you'd never heard him talk."

"You can tie up a domestic killing without my help," I said. "For you it's a daily crossword. All I did was —"

"If you say 'make a telephone call and knock on a door,' I'll leave you here with Burrough and Ransom and take a walk around the block. The FBI can make what it wants to out of it when it comes up for review."

He'd kept his temper, but then he'd had it on a leash so many years he knew he could whistle it back anytime he cut it loose. Only the bright whites of his eyes told you what would happen to you in between. I said, "I have to talk to the client."

"Do it now. You've got a cell."

I shook my head. "If the answer's no, you'll just confiscate it and check the log."

Burrough spoke up. "We can wait till the phone here's dusted, then you can use that. I got people checking on Bairn's location. Nothing else to do till they report, right, Inspector?"

I said, "Then you'll get the number from Ma Bell."

Alderdyce's face went as smooth as it could short of sandblasting. "Long distance, is it?"

"Yeah, you tricked it out of me. Narrows it down to the cops and the crooks and the people who can't afford to live outside this exchange."

"You live in it."

"Work it out. I'm not a cop and I don't have a record."

"Just a fistful of charges for withholding and obstruction. You've been behind bars so many times you've got grill marks on your ass."

"Can I quote you in my Yellow Pages ad?"

We went back into the kitchen. Officer Ransom's long bony face was flushed; he'd made a discovery. "Check out the calendar on the fridge, Inspector. This guy Bairn thinks it's September."

July and August were missing, including Bairn's scribbled appointment with Charlotte Sing, if that's what it was. Alderdyce looked. "Could be nothing," he said. "But good work, Officer."

The Mexican cleared his throat, almost too softly to hear.

"It was Ordoñez pointed it out," Ransom added, nearly as softly.

Alderdyce turned to the partner. "Why two pages, Officer?"

"In case somebody wrote something in July hard enough to make an indentation in August. Somebody's been watching Charlie Chan." The Mexican's smile withered short of full bloom.

"Well, like I said, it could be a dry hole." But Alderdyce sounded impressed. He looked at me. "I don't guess you noticed."

I shrugged and shook my head. This brought me into eye contact with Ordoñez. His were intelligent, mahogany-colored, and just as hard. He'd seen me looking at the calendar, all right; seeking it out. I'd led him right to it.

"Pick up your shit," Alderdyce told me. "Call that client you don't have. I don't hear from you by the end of the shift, you start the next in Holding."

Ransom said, "Sir, I know he's your friend —"

"Stand down, Officer," snapped Burrough.

Alderdyce addressed Ransom as if the detective hadn't interrupted. "He's a fucking hemorrhoid is what he is. But he's closed more police cases than you read in training. You learn to be half the cop he is, I'll put you in for plainclothes. You start to mouth off like him, I'll bust you down to khaki. Do like your partner, keep your trap shut and listen."

"Yessir." And an enemy was born.

I started scooping stuff back into my pockets. Alderdyce snatched up the envelope as I was reaching for it. "We'll hang on to this for now. You've got enough for gas."

"When do I get it back?"

"End of the shift." He smiled.

"How about a receipt?"

He looked at Burrough, who scribbled in his pad. When he hesitated before signing it, Alderdyce took the pad and mechanical pencil, scratched his name, tore out the sheet, and stuck it at me. I still have it:

Received from A. Walker: $50,000 cash.

I'm thinking of getting it framed.

Waiting for the attendant to pry my car out from behind a monster truck, I leaned against the plywood booth, the only shade in the lot, and tapped out a number on my cell. The signal went to a tower in the suburbs and from there to the ear of Darius Fuller, telling him he wasn't a father anymore. I listened to him gasping for breath, then mouthed the worthless words of sympathy and said the police would be in touch soon with details.

"What about you?" He sounded older than sixty now, dragging his glove back to the bullpen, beaten by the side.

"They want to know who I'm working for. If they see me with you, they'll know."

"It don't much matter now, does it?"

"I'd like to poke around a little. They've got Hilary Bairn all wrapped up for it, and maybe they're right. She was mad enough the last time I saw her to start a fight. But the cops don't know the whole story and it's not mine to tell."

"Why do you care? The job ended when — Oh, God." It broke then. You never know when it will or how bad. I took the telephone away from my ear until it subsided.

When it did I said, "There's something

else. If they find out what the job was and that you had a fight with Deirdre, it puts a whole new face on the investigation."

"You don't think they'll think it was me? She's my daughter, for Christ's sake!" Now he was mad.

"They know that. Pretty soon they'll know about the two million she had coming to her. Who gets it in the event she didn't live to collect?"

He paused. "Her heirs and assigns. If she didn't make other arrangements, that'd be me and Gloria. Her mother. Even split. What the hell are you saying?" Mad at me now. Hormones were colliding all over the place.

"I'm talking about the cops, not me. I just asked the question first. When they put the answer together with the fifty grand you gave me to pay him to walk away, they won't see it as a father's concern for his daughter's welfare. They're not paid to."

"You said it was an accident!"

"That's where the fight comes in. You didn't let it end there — where was it, by the way?"

"Here in the house, but —"

"You followed her to Bairn's place, they'll say, or went looking for her there. It started all up again. There was a scuffle. That's manslaughter, or at worst wrongful death. Money makes it something else. If the right one don't get you, the left one will. Prosecutor's dream."

"Jesus." It sounded like a prayer.

I paused. The attendant had brought up my car and got out to look at me, waiting for his money. He had a ball cap on backward and half a tin of Skoal under his lower lip. I stared at him until he turned, spat, and went into his booth. I walked a few yards away and lowered my voice. "There's something else."

"You already said that," Fuller said.

"The cops confiscated the fifty."

"Shit. Detroit cops? Shit."

"They're not all bent. I'll get it back, but if you tell them I'm working for you they'll reconstruct the whole thing like the archaeologists they are, and the rest will play out like I said."

"You're something," he said after a moment. "I don't know what, exactly, but when a man goes out of his way to tell someone not to help him stay out of jail, you got to trust him like a good catcher. How you figure to stay out long enough to do squat?"

"Same as always: Keep fouling 'em off till I get the pitch I want."

That was the end of the conversation. He

71

started to say something, choked, and clicked off after a second of dead air.

I hoped it wasn't an act. I was out on the same old dead limb and I didn't bounce as well as I used to.

Seven

When the day starts to run down there's no place like the office for a think. There are no clever decorative touches to distract the tired brain, no witchy PC to dangle the temptations of a walking tour of the hanging gardens of Babylon or a pornographic website in Milwaukee, no flashing lights on the telephone; just the same old dust-trap desk and file cabinets and scrap rug and flakes of cigarette ash waltzing in the current from the electric fan on the windowsill. The half-dozen other businesses that hung on three floors like leaves on a dead tree had closed for the day and down in the street the feral dogs crossed against the light without incident. Some of them still wore collars; the U of D and Wayne State University students had neglected to remove them when they turned their pets loose at the end of the term. The Dogs of Summer were a problem. They roamed in packs, scattering garbage, preying on small pets, and mauling children. Meanwhile the city had discontinued Animal Control on weekends to save money.

After I locked the door to the outer office I unzipped the compartment in the lining of my belt and took out the paper Darius Fuller had given me to have Bairn sign once money had changed hands. As evidence it was dynamite, and I couldn't count on the cops not making a more thorough search next time. The safe was good only for prop comedy. I opened a desk drawer, dumped the staples out of the stapler, gave the paper another fold lengthwise, and laid it in the narrow channel inside. I figured it would escape discovery unless someone decided to staple something.

I returned it to the drawer and put the swivel to work, with a glass in my hand and two inches of charcoal starter in the bottom. Soon it was in my stomach and the coals were warming up.

Deirdre Fuller was a sad surprise. If anyone had an early expiration date stamped on his forehead it was Hilary Bairn, who swiped expensive watches and tried to pawn them through his girlfriend to support his champagne tastes, which probably included gambling debts. Deirdre had survived celebrity parentage and a broken home, had two million dollars coming, and yet had still been studying for a profession. She'd smelled of sweet almonds, a scent I approved of in a world drenched in honeysuckle and lilac. I couldn't forget the expression on her face in Bairn's apartment, that look of weary acceptance that said she had the answers I needed.

One of them was what had happened to the watch. I hadn't seen it in either the kitchen or living room and Detective Burrough hadn't mentioned finding it in her handbag, a man's wristwatch in a woman's purse. If she'd gone there to confront Bairn over turning her into a fence for stolen merchandise, starting a fight that got her killed, it stood to reason she'd have had the evidence with her, to throw in his face. She wouldn't have tried to pawn it after the first time; love is blind, not stupid, and she hadn't the makings of a crook, not with an inheritance coming and her still committed to the law program at Michigan.

I could ask Bairn, if the cops didn't arrest him first. I'd start with where he went after he left the office early. Or I could ask Darius Fuller where *he* went after he fought with Deirdre at his house in Grosse Pointe. No wristwatch might mean she'd already said her piece to Bairn and he'd apologized and they were friends again and that was why she was waiting for him in his apartment. That would take the heat off the boyfriend. The father had sounded convincing on the telephone, but if her death was an accident he wouldn't have had to fake grief. It would also explain why no one else was home when the police investigated the disturbance. Most domestic killings are tied up on the spot, with the perpetrator waiting next to the corpse to be taken into custody. Intruders panic and leave.

I hoped it explained nothing. If it wasn't Bairn I hoped the case was a complicated one involving a mysterious hooded stranger and smuggled rubies, with parrots and a map and hot-air balloons and a Soviet sleeper agent who hadn't gotten the memo; cryptograms and bookcases that pivoted out to reveal secret passageways, or anyone or anything else but Darius Fuller. I'd gotten used to seeing sports heroes at their arraignments more often than on the field of play, but I liked it when parents didn't kill their children, even by accident. There wasn't liquor enough in the city for me to take on that kind of case.

The cigarette carton in the deep drawer of the desk was as empty as the pack in my pocket, and I'd only bothered to pick that up in case the forensics team found it in Bairn's apartment and thought it was a clue. They'd have plenty enough to go on once they lifted my fingerprints from places Bairn himself hadn't touched. That was going to cost me if I didn't have something to put on Inspector Alderdyce's desk before he went home at midnight. I tipped the carton into the wastebasket and got up to go out for more, and maybe a lead or something. I had all of six hours.

A telephone rang. Out of habit I lifted the receiver off the one on the desk and spoke my name into a dial tone. I put it down and broke loose the one on my belt.

"Is that Mr. Walker?" Female, with a musical sort of accent: Asian. When I said that was what it was, she said, "Please hold for Madame Sing."

I'd almost forgotten about her. The only reminder I'd had since I'd left my number with Victor Cho at the casino in Detroit Beach was the missing section from the calendar on Hilary Bairn's refrigerator, with her name scribbled in July. He might have gotten rid of it himself since that morning, or there might have been another notation in August that someone didn't want the cops to see; the name Sing had excited me so much I hadn't bothered to turn up the page. While I was waiting I tilted another inch into my glass and then into my mouth and rolled it around. It prickled my tongue like a tiny electric charge.

"Why Detroit Beach, Mr. Walker?" greeted another Asian voice, lower register, with the accent farther back. "I haven't been there in years."

I said, "I didn't expect to find you there. The joint's the closest one you've got to Bairn's place. If you had a debt to collect, that would be where he ran it up."

"I wouldn't know anything about that, Mr. Walker. I own real estate, not gambling houses."

"Are you saying Hilary Bairn didn't have an appointment to see you day before yesterday?"

"I have many appointments. I don't keep them all personally. I maintain assistants for less important meetings."

"Is that what Bairn was?"

"I don't know the gentleman."

"Victor Cho tried to stall me the same way. He made a mistake. He said, 'Who's he?' It's not a common name for men. Offhand the only other one I can think of is the man who climbed Mt. Everest; but that was his last name, so he doesn't count."

The pause on her end crackled with intelligence. "What is your interest?"

"This morning I needed background for a business proposition I was handling for a client. Tonight it's a criminal case. Bairn is being sought for questioning in a homicide."

"I wasn't aware private investigators involved themselves in police cases."

"Interesting."

"Yes?"

"That that would be the first thing you were curious about. Most people, when they hear the word homicide, want to know who was killed."

"The answer to that is irrelevant until I'm satisfied as to the reliability of the source."

I was beginning to understand her success. The vast majority of refugees who wash up on American shores vanish quickly into the soup, either dissolved into the stock or gathered in clumps with others of their nationality. Some float to the top all by themselves, others sink to the bottom and feed off the sediment. The ones who float to the top have to overcome prejudice, culture shock, barriers of language and custom, and all the usual forces that combine to prevent overcrowding at the highest level even among the natives. Charlotte Sing had had all that to contend with as well as her gender, yet had shot straight up from the sediment; if some of it still clung to her, you needed to have faced many of the same challenges to find fault, and even then you had to allow that she thought to ask the questions most people only assume they know the answers to.

I said, "If you don't know who I am by now, everything I've heard about you is an exaggeration."

"It probably is regardless. These things tend to take on a life of their own." She drew breath she didn't need. People like her — like me, too — prefer to have people think they're less certain than they are. "I've seen your military record, license renewals, marriage certificate and divorce decree, and a rather bloody swath through the local media. My privacy is more than just a comfort, Mr. Walker. Without it I can't function. I'm not convinced I can afford to involve myself with such a colorful character. In fact, I'm convinced I can't."

"It's me or the cops. They're not as gaudy, but their records are open to the public. And it isn't your backyard domestic homicide. The victim's father is a national celebrity."

"Would I know his name?"

"I think you already do. If I'm right about your calling in Bairn's markers, he'd have told you all about the money he's about to come into, to buy himself time. Two months, to be exact."

"Again you force me to embarrass myself with my ignorance. But if the story's that big, I won't need to take up my time and your minutes asking for details. When are you free tomorrow morning?"

"If it's tomorrow I won't be free at all, in every sense of the term. I need to see you tonight."

"One moment."

While on hold I grasped the bottle, then let it alone. I had an idea I'd need every cerebral cell I had left just to keep from falling any farther behind. After what seemed a long time she came back.

"I'm attending a private reception tonight at the Hilton Garden Inn, to celebrate some small effort I made to arrange an exhibition of preimperial Korean art at the DIA this fall."

"Is it formal? I keep my dinner jacket at a rental place downtown."

"You won't need it. You're not invited. I've taken a suite upstairs to dress. If you're there one minute past eight, you'll miss me."

"What's the number of the suite?"

"I don't know yet. My assistant isn't available. Ask for Mrs. MacArthur at the desk."

Detroit is never going to the Super Bowl, so it decided to invite the Super Bowl to Detroit. In order to prepare for fans from out of town, the Metro Convention and Visitors Bureau lured in outside investors to build 198 rooms in red brick in the old Harmonie Park neighborhood, close enough to walk to Ford Field — if the game didn't take place in February — and Comerica Park — if anyone cared to see how the Tigers were doing. The Hilton Garden Inn is the first hotel to go up in downtown Detroit since the Atheneum in 1993, but older ones built of better material with more style had been blown up in the meantime.

A pretty black girl in a sharp blazer greeted me at the desk. She didn't stir so much as a skin cell when I asked for Mrs. MacArthur, but the tone of her voice when she called up said everything it had to about a guest who would book a two-hundred-dollar suite just to change clothes. She cradled the receiver like Baby Jesus and gave me the number. She even provided directions to the elevator.

It lifted me without character to the top floor and let me out into a carpeted corridor that smelled like a new car, filled with future and promise and disinfectant. Recessed fixtures shed brushed-bronze light on pictures of milk wagons on Woodward and B-24s at Willow Run, Ty Cobb stealing a base, Tom Harmon throwing a pass, Isiah Thomas slamming a dunk; past and memory come in cans also. I followed scrolled brass numerals to an alcove at the end, and here I was, standing with knuckles raised in front of another door.

You can't work my job without becoming a connoisseur of doors, and a diviner of what was waiting on the other side: oak and stained glass — a kleptomaniac heir and a fat retainer; chipboard and printed veneer — a deadbeat dad and a rubber check; peeling paint — a cheating spouse and a tetanus shot; solid mahogany — an embezzler and a coverup; rusted screen — a shotgun and a running start. There were quaint Dutch doors that swung out in halves, seducing you with the smell of warm bread and a lonely restless woman at the oven; walnut-paneled doors that led you across fifteen feet of pile cuff-deep to a senior executive seated behind marble and glass, silver-haired, with a golden parachute and a stomach made of perforated tin; towering double-sided doors made from old-growth forest with Tiffany and Waterford in case lots behind them and no way to collect on what you had coming; steel-core doors, quilted on the reverse to lay the lunatic head against; swinging doors the orderlies bumped open with your gurney when you'd knocked on the wrong one; sliding doors, revolving doors, electric-eye doors, doors with bars, doors that moved up and down on tracks; doors that were just doors, something handy to push shut against a cancerous world, with bolts and latches and braces, and God help you if you came to it to ask for information, because it might come in the form of a forty-grain slug, fired by someone who was just a little more afraid than you were (see: swinging doors).

I'd stood in front of all of them at one time or another — behind them, too, in the case of the ones with bars — never without butterflies in my stomach, like a kid on his first Halloween; wondering if this was the Door To End All Doors, the one that would burst into yellow splinters and let a bullet tear into an organ I held dear.

This one, ordinary pine with an oak stain, felt something like that.

I didn't expect a bullet, really. Nothing so final and clear-cut. It was just a clammy mounting dread that came with the cold call, the blind search, the random shot, and the conviction that once I laid bone against wood, whatever I found on the other side would change the case, and probably my life. I'd listened to that warning whisper once already that same day and had walked away from it, surprising myself; only to keep my appointment in Samarra anyway when the cops sprang their trap.

So maybe the destiny people knew what they were talking about, and all this dithering was just a waste of my time and the client's money.

Nice pep rally. Give me a *W*.

I knocked. It opened. I didn't even duck.

EIGHT

"Mr. Walker? My name is Mai. I'm Madame Sing's personal assistant."

She had a little trouble with her *r*s and *l*s, but since I don't speak a second language myself I wasn't making judgments. She was a small creature in the prime middle years — no wrinkles, just a mature hardness in the lines of her cheeks — with black hair skinned back into a bun behind her head, in a pale yellow blouse with the square tail out over formfitting black slacks, tiny un-painted feet in open-toed pumps without heels, five feet and ninety pounds stripped and soaking wet. It might have been her voice I'd heard over the telephone; I'd been fooled once and so didn't jump to that conclusion.

"Am I early?"

"She'll be out in a minute. Please come in."

For all the chamber of commerce hysteria

about a new hotel in town, it was just a two-room suite like most, with a sitting room and a larger bedroom beyond. There was a king-size bed, made up tight as a trampoline with a quilted, peach-colored spread, a white faux Queen Anne desk with bowlegs, a fax machine, and all the necessary twenty-first-century ports, upholstered chairs and love seats, and identical black twenty-seven-inch TVs in both rooms. Prints on the walls with scenes of the Detroit riverfront and Impressionistic daubs of the Fox and State theaters. Fresh flowers erupted out of tall vases and a complimentary fruit basket done up in gold-tinted cellophane with a card in an envelope no one had bothered to open. The drapes were open, with a fine view of Harmonie Park and beyond it the music hall. From this side of the tinted Plexiglas it looked like a picture postcard, no indication of the punishing heat and general dearth of people.

"Would you like something to drink?" Mai made a gracious openhanded gesture toward the minibar, a half-grown refrigerator with a microwave oven on top. I said a Coke would be great.

"Not something stronger?"

"Okay, Mountain Dew."

She hesitated, smiling, eager to please.

"You are a detective, yes? You drink rye, with a bourbon chaser. I learn my English from Turner Classic Movies," she apologized.

I smiled. I wanted to wrap her up and set her on the mantel between the Balinese dancers. "Scotch, then. Do you have ice?"

"I can call down for some."

"Let's not bother them. They're only getting half a week's pay for one hour."

She laughed, an adorable little tinkly giggle like ceramic skulls banging together, and broke the hundred-dollar seal on the refrigerator door. The little plastic bottle of Glenlivet took up a cubic inch and a half of the glass she handed me. At least it was glass. When I was comfortable in a recliner with my drink she smoothed the front of her slacks and said, "Please excuse me while I check on her."

She went through a plain door behind which a hair dryer roared, mincing around the edge, and pushed it shut. I took a ten-dollar sip and then she came back out, reversing the movement. She walked as if her feet had been bound in infancy. "She'll be one minute. Shall I turn on the TV?"

"I bet you could, but let's not. These hotels get eighty channels and forty of them are *Designing Women.* What sort of boss is

Mrs. Sing to work for?"

"Madame Sing," she corrected. "She pays very well and she treats her employees with respect."

"Not like the Kyoto Health Spa out by the airport."

Her face went as dead as turned wood. "You only say that because I'm yellow."

"Partly. I admit it. In my work you judge by the folder and make adjustments as necessary. The rest is experience. You've got strong hands. The knuckles are splayed like a scrubwoman's, but smooth, with no dirt in the creases. That comes from working them in oil."

"Am I supposed to be impressed by your detective work?"

"Don't bother. The fact is you work for Charlotte Sing, who made her case dough from the massage business. A lot of these self-made millionaires make it a point to promote from within. I winged the rest. Except you do have strong hands."

"Eight hours a day at a computer keyboard will do that, too. But if you want to discuss hand jobs — yes, I know the basics. Another?" she said brightly.

I followed her gaze to my empty glass. I didn't remember drinking. I said no thanks and set it on a table.

Just then the dryer stopped howling. At the end of a loud silence the bathroom door opened and a woman came out wearing paper slippers and a terry robe. She was as small as her assistant; the fluffy white material wrapped around her nearly twice and brushed her insteps. Her hair was cut straight across her eyebrows in blue-black bangs, dyed probably, and stopped abruptly at the corners of her jaws. She was about the same age as the other woman but showed it more in the beginnings of jowls and lines in her neck. She looked at me without smiling, then at the assistant. "Mai, please go in and check my dress for wrinkles. They should be steamed out by now, but if not, you'll need to run the shower a bit longer."

"Yes, Madame." She went into the bathroom and pushed the door to.

"Alone at last." I grinned.

The woman didn't. "You fulfill the common expectations of an American detective. Which raised my suspicions. Most things genuine aren't what you expect. May I see your credentials?"

I gave her the flapper. "Ignore the badge. I only carry it for ballast."

She slid the photo card out of its window, inspected both sides, and put it back. My concealed weapons permit was folded inside and she took that out too and unfolded and read it, front to back, then returned it. "Are you armed at present?"

"No. It didn't seem like that kind of hotel."

"Unconvincing."

"Frisk me. While you're at it, I've got a touch of bursitis in my left shoulder."

But she didn't anger that easily. "I meant this." She stuck out the folder between two fingers. "There's a laser shop on every corner, and the card isn't a challenge to duplicate to begin with. Anyone can obtain permission to carry a gun in this state if he doesn't have a criminal record."

"On the other hand," I said, pocketing the folder, "who'd want to impersonate an American detective?"

"Tell me about the Fuller killing."

"So you did look it up."

"Mai did. It was just breaking. There weren't many details. Are you working for Hilary Bairn? You said you had a proposition for him, but that could have been a Trojan horse."

I reached over and circled a finger inside my empty glass. It gave off a flat hum. It looked like fine crystal, but appearances aren't the test. "I'm saving that answer for

Mrs. Sing."

Her face gave me nothing, not even a hum.

I said, "It was a clever switch. The dress thing was a little clumsy. You don't need a home wrinkle remedy in a hotel with a valet service. Her voice is a little deeper, with less accent, but you both did a good job of disguising the differences. Anyway, I fell for that once today, so I disregarded it as evidence. But I was already wise. You lost me at the door."

"At the door? But —" She interrupted herself to glance toward the bathroom. It was the first crack in the smooth surface.

"Mai is a Vietnamese name," I said. "She's Korean. I spent three years shooting at your relatives and getting shot at by them." I licked the Scotch off my finger and waggled it at her. "You knew that, Mai. You looked me up for your boss."

Her voice went up a register. "I don't —"

"It's all right, Mai," Charlotte Sing said. "Will you fix me a drink, please?"

She'd ditched the coolie rig and came out dressed for the evening in deep, dragon's-blood garnet, with bare shoulders and a slit in the skirt that exposed her sheer hose to mid thigh. She looked taller in heels, had an athletic figure, and whoever she'd gone to to swindle the forces of gravity hadn't left any scars or folds. In that outfit the skinned-back hairstyle looked aristocratic, not just something to keep her hair out of her eyes while she took dictation. She looked younger and more confident.

I tested that. "You made the same mistake before, when you said you all looked alike to us. It backfired and made you famous."

"Another prejudice gone. We aren't all infallibly intelligent. Thank you, Mai." She accepted a glass poured from a pony bottle of vodka and a can of Canada Dry. "This time it wasn't a joke. The variety of ways the authorities have sought to entrap me is infinite. Sometimes the seams are easier to detect from an oblique angle."

"Watching and listening," I said. "When they're watching and listening to someone else."

"It's all very time-consuming. You can see why I hide."

"Nice camouflage."

She glanced down at her dress. "If I don't make an appearance now and then, I risk becoming an enduring mystery. They'd never let me alone."

Mai hovered. "Do you need me to take notes?"

"Go in and get dressed. I won't need you anymore tonight."

She glanced back at me, not so sure of that. But she went into the bathroom and shut the door.

"How much can she hear?" I asked.

"Everything. She's very dependable. And very confidential."

"You're paying her, I'm not. I'll wait. Okay if I raid the refrigerator?"

"Be my guest." There was a love seat perpendicular to the chair. She made herself comfortable, crossing the exposed leg over the other and sipping from her glass, while I found the last bottle of Glenlivet and filled mine the rest of the way from the can of ginger ale. It's a terrible thing to do to a premium label, but I hadn't eaten and she was smarter than a fresh coat of varnish. I took my time, stirring it with a plastic straw from the coffee setup on the low bureau, until Mai emerged in the clothes her boss had been wearing and let herself out of the suite. When the door snicked I went out to make sure she hadn't hung back and to double-lock it. When I returned to the bedroom, Charlotte Sing said, "Are you always this careful, or are you showing off?"

"A little of both. I've got just over four hours before I have to give up my client's name or something of equal or greater value to the cops, and if Mai gets to them first with the same information, my bargaining chip's busted; they'll say I dragged my feet and find something else to hold me on just on principle. If I'm a little flashy about the precautions, you'll get the point a lot stronger than if I just told you it was important."

"You may be right. If I hadn't seen it, I wouldn't have thought it possible for anyone to be more circumspect than I am."

I stepped over and touched my glass to hers. Then I sat down. "I'm working for Darius Fuller, the dead woman's father. He hired me to pay Bairn fifty thousand dollars to get out of her life."

"I understood Fuller's in bankruptcy."

"There's broke and broke. Bairn stood to share in a two-million-dollar trust fund if he married Deirdre Fuller. If you're the romantic type, you could say he loved his daughter and wanted whoever married her to do it for her, not her money."

"But I am the romantic type," she said. "My life is a romance, if you overlook the X rating. I'm also a businesswoman. Why settle for a candle when you can have the whole cake?"

"Time, for one. He had creditors pushing him for cash now. The pressure must have been tight, because he took the chance of

95

blowing his relationship with Deirdre by conning her into trying to pawn a watch he'd shoplifted somewhere."

"Darius begins to look like Father of the Year. Why didn't Bairn pawn the watch himself?"

"The obvious answer is he'd tried it before, with other merchandise, and got his hand smacked the same way a broker in Ypsi smacked hers when she tried it there. Those fellows run a tight network. They don't mess with cops if they can avoid it, and contrary to popular opinion they'd rather do business than break bones. When they catch you trying to fence something, they pin you down, take your picture, and blanket all the shops in the area with copies. I assume now they subscribe to a Web site or something and save postage. If that happened to Bairn, he needed a ringer. If you're deep enough in Dutch to try to scam the pros, it stands to reason you're fresh out of friends who'll do it for you. That left Deirdre."

"How much of this is established fact?"

"The important part. The watch part. The rest is speculation based on observation. What I came here to find out is what you did that scared him so badly he'd risk a sure two million to get you off his back."

I didn't expect her to throw herself to the

floor and chew through to the suite below, but what she did was almost as satisfying. She lifted her glass and took a sip. Before it had been just a prop. Now she needed something to break eye contact; not to conceal guilt, just a change in body temperature that would prove she was made of organic material like the rest of us.

"Again, you've mistaken the properties I own for what stands upon them. You should be having this conversation with Victor Cho. If Mr. Bairn owes money in Detroit Beach, he'd be the one to collect."

"Bairn's appointment was with you, not Cho."

"Did Bairn tell you that?"

"His apartment did. I'm not trying to entrap you, Mrs. Sing. Now that the state and the city are in the gambling business, I don't care who blows the rent money where. I'm only interested in staying out of jail."

"By attempting to put me there in your place?"

"They don't have to know anything about this conversation. They're all fired up to charge Bairn with manslaughter, but I complicated things by calling him on his phone and knocking on his door. All I have to do is convince them the job I was doing for Darius Fuller hasn't anything to do with what happened to his daughter."

"How do you know that?"

"That part's trickier. I have to convince myself first."

She stood her glass on the nightstand beside the bed and sat back, or at least returned to upright; her back never touched the cushions. "If I said Bairn came to me for help, a stranger with means who'd known her share of hardship and injustice, would you accept that, purely as a hypothesis?"

"I might try it for a block or two. I'm not sure how a load like that would hold turning a corner."

"There would, naturally, be compensation down the line for my assistance."

"The problem would be confirming it. It wouldn't be like Deirdre Fuller signed a contract promising to marry him and make him her mutual beneficiary."

"That would not be the problem, because the request would be refused. The return would be usurious, and would play directly into the hands of those individuals who have taken an unhealthy interest in my future. It's very exhausting, the number of directions they find to come at me. Am I so tempting a target, in a world full of terrorists and drug dealers?"

"You're a headline. Offer a public prosecutor money and he'll put you in the pokey, but a teaser at the top of the news will get you the liquor concession in the City-County Building. The lawyer who bags Charlotte Sing can be the next governor." I changed hands on my glass. "So when you turned Bairn down, killing his last best hope, he slid back into old habits."

"He might have, if the conversation had actually taken place."

"Yeah. Do you mind if we switched tenses? I always had trouble with subjunctive."

"As long as it's understood we're still speaking in generalities. Even an innocent and indirect connection to an accidental killing would expose me to publicity, and the cycle would begin all over again."

"Did he mention who was putting the screws to him?"

She regarded me, an exotic cat with fangs covered and claws retracted.

"Wilson Watson," she said. "I think that was the order. Interchangable Christian names challenge me. Are you familiar with it?"

"I would be." I sucked hard at my drink, trying to separate the alcohol from the fizz.

NINE

"He's a gangster," she said.

"Labor leader, he says. Do you know him?"

"We have a mutual acquaintance in Victor Cho. Watson's been trying to organize workers in unlicensed casinos for years. Cho's had his agitators forcibly ejected several times. This is hearsay. The only interest I have in any of the establishments that operate on my property is the rent."

"He tried the same thing in the licensed joints in Detroit, but the gaming commission won't let him in the door. He has a felony record going back to the sixty-seven riot. If he comes within five hundred feet of a legitimate gambling operation, back to jail he goes."

"How does one dictate wages and benefits to an enterprise that's criminal to begin with?"

"With clubs and axes and the occasional

unexplained fire. Did Bairn say how Watson got his hooks in?"

"He did, but it was hard to follow. He went broke at Detroit Beach and went to an outside automatic teller machine for cash, which he lost also. The next thing he knew, Watson's people were pressuring him. Is it possible for a private individual to operate his own ATM?"

"Possible. Not legal. They buy obsolete machines at auction, retrofit them to their own specifications, and put them up in public places. People think they're with-drawing their own money, but they're really giving up their account numbers and PINs to a stranger. Looks like in Watson's case he'd rather soak them like some state-of-the-art loan shark than just clean them out once like an honest thief. You can steal someone's whole life with just those two little numbers. You don't even have to threaten to break his fingers if he doesn't pay. It's a new racket. Up till now he's made his money collecting dues from casino em-ployees who can't work in the straight places, and squeezing the crooked places for protection. The union only exists in the owners' worst nightmares."

"Nothing about it sounded right, so I gave Mr. Bairn my regrets. The only reason he came to me is the delusion I'm actually involved in Detroit Beach." She glanced at a tiny diamond watch strapped to the underside of her wrist. "I must be on my way. I'm sorry I couldn't be more helpful."

"I doubt you are. But you put a face on the dragon." When I stood up, a hollow gong struck inside my head. The liquor was kicking in. I needed to float something in it before I bearded someone like Wilson Watson. "Thanks very much for your time."

She remained seated. "I was curious to see what kind of snare they were setting for me this time. I'm happy I was mistaken. I'll hold on to your card. Mai told me you sometimes do security work. Would you consider a temporary position on my staff next time I travel?"

"I thought you only employed Asians."

"I prefer to, when their abilities match or excel those of the occidentals who apply. As a businesswoman I can't afford to dismiss anyone out of hand on the basis of race alone. I'm not a university."

"Would the job include carrying your bags?"

"No. I have people for that, as well as for the bags belonging to the security personnel. A bodyguard with his hands full is useless."

"How do they get their guns aboard the planes?"

"The planes are chartered. I stopped taking commercial flights after nine-eleven. I'm not concerned about fanatics, but I dislike being ordered about by cocktail waitresses."

"I get five hundred a day."

"I think I can do a little better. Of course, travel, meals, and accommodations are included."

"When's your next trip?"

"Sometimes I have to leave on two hours' notice."

"Heat?"

"Fluctuations in the market."

"I'll start carrying a toothbrush in my pocket." I hung back at the door connecting to the sitting room. "I know why you have to register under a pseudonym. But why MacArthur?"

Her smile belonged on a silk print with ponds and pagodas.

"Sentiment. He was the first American to leave Korea."

Wilson Watson was one of those names, like Twelfth and Clairmount, that brought back memories most Detroiters who lived through the period would rather burn, bury, and cover with salt. He was seventeen in

103

1967, hauling around a string of juvenile offenses already, when a police raid on a blind pig on that corner touched off the granddaddy of all race riots, with pistols and Molotov cocktails on one side and M-60 tanks on the other. Forty-three people died, 1,383 buildings burned, and the phrase "soul brother" entered the national lexicon, having been spray painted on black-owned businesses in hopes of sparing them from the torch — in vain, by and large. Once a city of a million starts rolling downhill, racial ties alone won't slow it down.

Of the nearly four thousand people arrested that week, Wilson Watson was among the first. He'd organized a band of looters who made their way systematically across the smoldering city, across the wounded, wailing city, targeting savings and loan offices, electronics outlets, and liquor stores and removing cash and merchandise that could be liquidated easily. A number of witnesses summoned to testify against him at his trial vanished or lost their memories on the stand, but those who cooperated with the prosecution gave evidence that Watson had set out to raise money to import high-grade heroin from Asia and the Middle East and squeeze out the independents. He'd gotten the Call, which was to become the biggest drug czar in the Great Lakes. The authorities, shell-shocked and uncomfortably aware of the disparity between a predominately white police department and an overwhelmingly black community, were inclined to deal leniently with the common run of portable TV thieves, but Watson was a hard-shell criminal and an opportunist with an agenda. A judge sentenced him as an adult to twenty years at hard labor for his ambition. He served only eleven, despite getting caught placing bets on the 1968 World Series through his attorney, who was disbarred shortly thereafter.

The friendships you form in prison are the longest lasting. In return for teaching him that the gambling culture offered a higher return for less risk than narcotics, the acquaintances Watson made while inside found employment for life with his organization when they were released. His business manager was a convicted rapist, whose junkets on his superior's behalf were made more complicated by his need to register himself as a sex offender everywhere he went. His personal security was unchanged from the circle of meat-brained weight lifters who'd protected him in the yard, and he retained the services of his disgraced lawyer as an unofficial legal consultant. His front man, who knew which fork to use at a formal dinner and never wore silk with tweeds, was a murderer; his responsibility was to pay the initial visit to an unlawful casino whose employees lacked union representation. According to legend, Ernesto Esmerelda carried a black steel toolbox containing a hammer and three-inch spikes, which he'd had to use only once to nail a reluctant manager's hand to his desktop. After the story got around, the sight of the box alone tended to bring out the desired result. If Victor Cho was as stubborn about meeting with Watson's shop stewards as Charlotte Sing had said, he'd have been wise to keep his hands off his desk when Esmerelda came calling.

There is an Ernesto Esmerelda in every case, although often the name is less ethnic, and his choice of tools varies. He was my candidate for the unnamed representative who'd taken Hilary Bairn to task for his withdrawals from one of Watson's private ATMs. He was a Cuban national, a member of a pre-Castro aristocratic family and a veteran of the Mariel boatlift, who'd smuggled himself back into the U.S. after deportation following his release from the state prison in Jackson. A garden-variety killer and strong-arm specialist fell fairly low on the list for attention from Homeland Security, which was more interested in Islamic terrorists this season. He would be a very old man on oxygen before INS got around to picking him up and sending him back. If it came to a firefight, Esmerelda was the one you took out first, if you were quick enough and not overconcerned with contracting a mortal wound in the doing. I was pretty sure we'd meet.

What had started out as a simple business proposition with a little implied intimidation had taken a sharp left turn into organized crime. And wasn't that always the way?

I needed something in my stomach before I forced a meeting with Wilson Watson. There was a Burger King not far from the Hilton Garden Inn, and I fortified myself with a bacon cheeseburger, fries, and a full-leaded Coke on the way back to the office, where I looked up the number of the front he was using that year, a tool-and-die shop in Warren. The perky receptionist I got there had never heard of Watson, but took down my cell phone number without making any promises. I told her my business had to do with Deirdre Fuller. She asked me to spell both names.

"Have you got a TV in the office?"

She hesitated. "Yes."

"Turn it on, any channel. You'll see it pretty soon."

After that there was nothing to do but swallow the bitter pill and call Darius Fuller. I had a little over two hours before I turned back into a church mouse and had to report to the head cat at the cophouse.

"Yeah, man." He sounded played out, and mellow from something that didn't necessarily come in bottles. I asked if the police were there.

"They left a little while ago. Nice boys, sympathetic. No guarantee they'll stay that way."

"They ask about Bairn?"

"Yeah. I told them the situation with Deedee; the fight, everything. Nice boys, didn't bat an eye when I mentioned the two million. I don't think either one of them was old enough to see me pitch."

"They hatch full-grown. Did you tell them about our arrangement?"

"No. They didn't ask."

"Want me to sit on it?"

A long breath got drawn with a rattle in it. "Oh, who the hell cares? Give 'em what they want. They'll be back anyway."

"Maybe not the same ones. It may be an

inspector named Alderdyce and a detective named Burrough." I let three seconds of silence tumble down the line. "There's more to the story."

"Figured there would be." He didn't sound curious.

"I don't need to tell the cops any more than they ask, but do you want me to come up there first and bring you up to code? It doesn't tell over the phone."

"Not tonight, okay? I got arrangements to make starting early tomorrow, and I don't know when they'll let me have the — have Dee-dee." He breathed again. "I got to call her mother. I don't mind telling you I'm not looking forward to it."

"Sure. Can I come see you tomorrow when it's done?"

"Am I still paying you?"

"Not if you say no."

"We'll talk about it. Call first. I got to the end of the month to be out of here, but I don't think I can stand it that long. There's no furniture, and everywhere I look she fills the space. Shouldn't, she hasn't lived here since she was little. You know?"

"I don't know, but I can guess."

"Thanks for that." He sounded sincere. "First fucker tells me he knows just how it is gets the high hard one straight in the mouth."

I said nothing. That seemed to be expected.

"I got one credit card I didn't max out," he said. "I been saving it. Think I'll blow it on a hotel room. That old sleeping bag's not much to put between the floor and these old bones."

"The suites at the new Hilton aren't bad."

"It's too close to the new ballpark. I never did forgive the club for giving up on The Corner and selling out to a fucking financial institution. I lost my eighty-four Series bonus in that whole S-and-L deal."

"You should've stuck with baseball."

"Tell that to my arm. Sooner or later everything you depend on goes away." He swallowed something. "Call. I'll tell you where you can find me."

"Sure you want to be alone tonight?"

"Sure as hell. I don't expect to be again for a long time."

His voice was getting guttural. I said okay and got off the line. When I got back on it to check for messages, the connection was still open. I heard air stirring in an empty room. When I tried again after a minute the dial tone came on, so he must have found the cradle with the receiver finally.

Dusk was crumbling in. I shut down the

plant and put wheels under me. In a little while Greektown came up, always open, the bluebottle and pink popsicle lights of the tribal casino spilling out of Trappers Alley, an appropriate name if ever there was one, and beyond it the rotting hulk of 1300 Beaubien — Detroit Police Headquarters — rising like a ruined redoubt from the fog that prowled in from the river when the mercury slipped. I found a spot for the car and went inside to make my offering.

TEN

I found John Alderdyce in his office, glowering at a plastic bucket collecting drips from a reservoir stagnating in the crawl space between his ceiling and the floor above. No rain had fallen for two weeks, but at 1300 it's always monsoon season. Eighty years of indifferent use, with two decades of corruption at city hall, had turned a proud local landmark into a leaky hut in Thailand. Overhead, the entire seventh story was deserted, evacuated by order of a former chief because of rotten ventilation, sagging plaster, rats, black mold, and pigeon filth.

"I like what you've done with the place," I said.

He gave up trying to stare a hole through the bucket and started on me. "You hear where they're planning to put us now?"

"Belle Isle? They're shutting down the aquarium. Everyone gets a window."

"The Michigan Central Depot. It's ten

years older than this dump, with bats."

"Use them instead of the silhouette targets. Ten or better to qualify."

He pointed a scarbound knuckle at the school clock on the wall. "Your watch is fast."

"I thought I was cutting it kind of close."

"That's what I meant. I had the arrest report all typed, with blanks for resisting and getting shot trying to escape."

"End of the shift, you said. I knew you'd still be here. You never shave a minute off city time." I lifted the bucket, catching the water while I slid the chair out from under it and set the bucket on the floor. The seat was damp when I sat down. The leak had gotten a head start.

The telephone rang on his desk. He let it go until someone got it on an extension or the caller gave up. He was sitting in his old brown-and-yellow plaid chair with his hands resting on the arms where all the pattern had worn off. He watched me through the holes in his skull without moving. Water dripped into the bucket without any rhythm or pattern: Plinkety-plunk splat bloop plunketa-plink gurgle smack. Taking down the old building with it, a gram at a time.

"Darius Fuller," I said.

He clapped his hands once. It sounded

like a shot.

I said, "The fifty grand was to offer Bairn to walk away from the daughter. You know about the two million she had coming on her next birthday."

"Bairn's a bookkeeper. Didn't Fuller think he knew six zeroes beats four of a kind?"

"That was my end. I was supposed to make mean faces and crack my knuckles while he considered."

"Muscle now, is it? Times are harder than I thought."

"Not that hard, and I told Fuller so. It didn't change his mind. Later I found out some things about Bairn that told me he might like the walking-around money now as opposed to waiting two months to inherit the ranch."

"Who's he owe, and how hard are they leaning?"

"I didn't get that far." My voice throbbed with truth. "He tried to raise cash by conning Deirdre Fuller into hocking a hot watch."

"Rolex?"

"My guess. I didn't get that close. Anyway the pawnbroker threw it in her face, so I figured Bairn for an easier fall than he looked at the start. Then the situation changed again."

"The daughter threatened to move up the wedding date. My officers got that from Fuller. She sprang it on him, he said, while they were arguing about Bairn. You know this gives him two motives for her killing, both biblical."

"Wrath and greed," I said. "Worst of the seven. You really like him for it?"

"*Like* doesn't figure in. I'd *like* it if everyone who ever got murdered just ran into the wrong stranger on the wrong corner. Then it's just a matter of following leads, collecting evidence, and baling it all up for the prosecutor. Clean and clinical, like a scientist isolating a virus. I could wear white. But the killers don't care what I like. Two thirds of the complaints that roll across this desk have to do with husbands killing wives, children killing parents, parents killing children. It happens we're having our hottest summer in years, with brownouts fucking up the air conditioners in those houses that have them. That rachets up the rage factor, and since there are more guns in Detroit than in Texas, a fight that in November might lead to a black eye winds up here on my desk. I'm looking forward to the first frost. Do I *think* Fuller did it? No, even though he's got no alibi for how he spent the next several hours after he and

Deirdre had words in Grosse Pointe. *He* says he got got drunk and passed out on his sleeping bag because his bed got sold. The officers who spoke with him there smelled marijuana, which helps to corroborate his story rather than tear it down. I never worked a passion killing yet that was committed under the influence of that kind of depressant."

"That leaves the two million and premeditation. The weed slows down your thinking. Some people think that makes it clearer."

"Musicians, mostly." He shook his head. "He never struck me as greedy when he played ball. I remember once the club offered him a hundred grand back when that was money for a professional athlete, and him going through a slump, with a wife and a mortgage and a mother in a nursing home. He turned it down; told them to give him half and save the rest for someone who'd had a better year. People change for the worse when they change at all, but to me that story earns him the benefit of the doubt."

"I always said you were too softhearted for this job."

"Fuck you. I can still take you down for withholding six hours at the beginning of an investigation when they count most. You already missed supper at County. It was corned beef."

"I know. The chef could work anywhere if he didn't keep breaking parole. I still think you're a pussycat. What's Bairn got to say for himself?"

"I'll ask him when he turns up. He left the office early today and nobody's seen him since. In this business we call that part of a suspicious pattern. We've got a BOLO out on him and his car, an asshole-ugly orange Aztek. Him I like for it," he said. "He went home, found her waiting to jump him about the stolen watch, and events took their usual course. In those cases we usually find the guy waiting to confess, but not always. Bairn sounds like a runner to me, and a prick to boot. There won't be a wet eye in the courtroom when he goes down for Man One."

"So you figure Deirdre was running a bluff when she told Darius they were getting married right away."

"Had to be. She was already pissed off at herself for getting mixed up with a petty thief and a fortune hunter, so she lashed out at the old man when he said pretty much the same thing. Part of being family means knowing just where to hit to cause the most pain. She had plenty of steam left when she confronted the boyfriend and broke off the relationship."

"Why Man One? Any halfway decent lawyer can plead a case like that down to second-degree. Bairn was too desperate over his own situation to think before he struck."

"We already know he was behind on his rent. I called the MGM Grand and Motor City and Greektown; that's SOP in this kind of scenario. He's banned from them all for bouncing checks for his losses. They put collection agencies on him and there are two court orders pending to garnish his wages. His boss at the medical courier place turned him down on an advance. You have to guess he tried his luck with the sharks and illegal clip joints around town, and their collection agencies don't bother with the courts. I'd say he was desperate." He drummed his fingers on the arms of his chair. "Only thing that keeps this whole theory from being a slam dunk is forensics."

I was playing with a cigarette. You can't smoke there anymore so I hadn't lit it. I put it carefully back in the pack. "It wasn't a blow to the temple?"

"ME's prelim didn't find anything to dispute it. She has a contusion in the right place for a cerebral hemorrhage or subdural hematoma, which picks its time according to the force of the blow. Sweepsters came up negative on skin cells on the metal lamp shade and all of the other surfaces she might have come into contact with when she fell or was pushed. A fist might do it, but I've never run across a fatal case except once at Joe Louis Arena."

"Ring injury?"

He nodded. "You have to hit hard in just the right spot. Frankly, I don't think Bairn had the horsepower."

"Blunt instrument?"

"The ME will know for sure when he peels back the flap. Nothing in the apartment tested for the weapon, which meant he carried it away with him. That complicates a plea for second-degree."

For no particular reason I thought about a beanball. I recalled Darius Fuller being ejected a time or two for throwing at a batter's head. I stopped thinking about it. To begin with it was stupid, but I'm also superstitious about cooking up theories against a client in the presence of experienced police officials. They read minds.

"Did the watch turn up?" I asked.

"I didn't see it in the inventory, either from the apartment or at work. His boss let us look. It would more or less make our case if we find it in his possession. She'd likely have had it with her when she jumped him, and it would put him on the scene. That's if they hadn't already had that conversation earlier, in which case we can't even show they fought today."

I spread my hands. "Are we good?"

He said nothing while the rain bucket improvised new chords. Then he opened a drawer and flipped a familiar envelope onto the desk. It made a smack. "We're good. Until I have to come back to you for what you're still sitting on." He watched me pick up the envelope. "You might want to count the bills."

"You I trust." I put it in an inside pocket.

"You'd be screwing yourself. I slipped in an extra twenty. You won the bet. Mary Ann Thaler called. She got the job. Going to hold hands with snitches for the U.S. Marshals."

ELEVEN

At the end of the first full day on the job I didn't know if I had one. That added to the exhaustion. I took down the bottle from the cupboard over the sink where it had been cooking all day in the lack of air-conditioning, poured the contents over ice, and watched the cubes on top spontaneously combust in a cloud of steam. The ones on the bottom cracked and shifted like tectonic plates. The liquor tasted like ammonia, but I hadn't chosen the label for the flavor. In a little while I got undressed, slid between the sheets, and rode the mattress until I slept. My tolerance was on the retreat. One collateral benefit of growing older is it doesn't cost as much to get drunk.

In the morning, pooch-eyed and hollow, I filled and turned on the coffee machine and took a tepid shower. It was seventy-five out already and as I toweled off, last night's dew was lifting outside the window like a glassine curtain. A silver Hummer brumbled past, looking like an Erector Set on wheels; I felt its sonic system under my feet all the way from the upper end of Joseph Campau. Slumming, from Birmingham or Bloomfield Hills or the Pointes. The first month's payment alone would get you a crib well outside the Detroit zip code.

It came back the other way as I was dressing. From the bedroom window I could see the driver craning his neck, reading addresses. He hadn't much to crane. His head in profile sat like Stonehenge square on his shoulders. At the end of my driveway he came to a full stop, then backed up to make the turn. He still managed to bump a rear tire over the curb, leaving a waffle-patterned impression for future paleontologists to puzzle over. For a full minute after he braked, no one came out. The big bass speakers in the back continued pumping, rocking the body on its springs with each downstroke and radiating vibes through the bedrock under Hamtramck and the city that surrounded it.

I didn't like it and I hadn't a gun in the house. The Chief's Special was at the office and I'd left the Luger in the car. A serious oversight, given the turn the case was taking, but I could punish myself for it later, if

I lived. When the door opened on the driver's side and a foot came down — a foot in a size-fourteen boot with flames on the toes, stepping right past the hammered-steel tread for climbing up and down — I went back to the kitchen, poured a cup of coffee, and took the steaming carafe with me when the doorbell rang. Scalding liquid is better than no gun at all, especially if you go for the eyes.

The eyes would have been a reach. Normal-size doorways would always be a challenge for this one. He wore a gray hoodie sweatshirt — in that heat — with yellow lettering on the front that informed me someone very large had attended the Rhode Island School of Engineering and Design. I couldn't tell if he was black or white. He had flat features that might have been Polynesian, or the result of some miscue in the genetic code, and his skin was cinnamon. Little patches of scar tissue like tape adhered to the corners of his eyes. His big heavy-veined hands hung at his sides with the fingers curled. His elbows bent slightly; shortening of the tendons caused by overtraining with weights. I was going to have to put on a second pot to make any sort of dent.

One of the hands came up. I stepped back

to get a good swing with the carafe, but he was only looking at a scrap of paper stuck between his thumb and forefinger. "Your number's down." His voice was shallow and a little high, a waste of all that room in his chest. "Right place for Walker?"

"That's a matter of opinion."

He chuckled. That floored me. I wouldn't have thought even a good joke would make it through all that muscle and bone. "Yeah. The girl in the office said you weren't long on straight answers."

"Which girl and which office?"

"Tracy. ABC Tool and Die?"

I'd half worked it out before he gave me the name of Wilson Watson's front in Warren, but I'd wanted to make sure. Watson was a small man physically who liked to surround himself with big men, like Stalin, and had done all his recruiting from the Mr. Universe block at Jackson. Between the weights and the steroids smuggled in by crooked guards, it was a wonder this one hadn't just pushed down the west wall.

I said, "I've always wondered. What does a tool and die shop do?"

"I don't know. I never been inside and neither has Wilson. We can come in, right?"

He was the least pushy strongarm I'd ever met and the closest to polite. He was a big dog you could lay your head on and listen to its heart thump in its deep hollow chest, that could gobble you up bones and all. "We meaning you? You're big, but you don't qualify for a group rate."

He turned a quarter inch and made some kind of gesture. I couldn't see it because he still filled the door. A car door thunked, gravel crunched. The eclipse passed. When his tame elk stepped aside, Wilson Watson hopped up onto the front stoop.

He was short, a round torso perched on spindles that turned out at the knees, a textbook example of a vitamin A deficiency in early childhood. He wore an eight-ball jacket that made me sweat to look at it, a suede cap with the bill cocked over his left ear, and black leather pants swiped from the fashion department at Toys 'R' Us, two hundred bucks of NBA advertising on his feet, which were the largest thing about him and turned out also, anchoring him to the ground. He looked like one of those stuffed lacquered frogs they prop up on their hind legs and sell in souvenir shops, holding fishing poles or strumming little guitars.

My poker face must have slipped, because a pair of yellow eyes stared up at me from a round puddle of medium-brown skin with a stringy Fu Manchu moustache and a tiny pubic patch in the hollow of the chin. "The fuck you gawking at?"

"I just got out of bed. I dreamed the eighties were over."

"Funny joke," explained the big man to the side of the door. "Man don't know from retro."

"Let's inside. You got Zima?"

"Scotch and beer," I said. "I'm not sure about the Scotch. It's got a Little Rock accent."

"That went out with Reagan. Just pour me a cup of shit."

I realized then I was still holding the coffeepot. Outside, the Hummer's speakers were still humping the frame. Between percussions the engine continued to idle. "You should lock up your ride. The neighborhood's on the downhill run."

The big man spoke up. "Wilson's name's on the plate. That's way better than the Club."

I stepped out of the path and Watson crab-walked inside, swinging his arms for momentum and setting each foot square with a loud slap. The temperature dropped five degrees as his companion dragged his shade over me, following. The big man swiveled his head from side to side on the way through the living room. "I was wrong," he said. "The man do know from retro."

"It was all new when I brought it home."

Watson went straight through to the kitchen, which said something about his background, and sat down in the little breakfast nook. The heavy lifter didn't even try. He stood in front of the refrigerator, just another major appliance, with his arms bent and the scrap of paper with my address still in one hand. He seemed to have forgotten he had it.

I plonked a mug down in front of his boss. "How do you take it?"

"Black as my ass."

The big man grinned. "You ask, he'll show you."

I was starting to like him. I asked him what his name was.

"Ain't got one," Watson said. "I never have to call him, he's right there all the time."

"Elron," the big man said. "My mother was a Scientologist."

I said, "I think that's L. Ron, with an initial. L. Ron Hubbard, founder of the Church of Scientology. You know he wrote science fiction."

"So what? Mohammed wrote poetry."

"I didn't know that."

"I studied all the religions, Scientology's still the best. I knew about L. Ron, so did

127

my mother. Clerk that filled out the birth certificate was a Southern Baptist."

I liked him. I wondered where I could hit him that wouldn't break my hand.

Watson watched me fill his mug, then get out two more. "Don't bother watering Elron. He only drinks protein, straight from the jug."

"Leetle powdered creamer," Elron said. "Nondairy."

"Sorry. All I've got is milk."

"That tears up my stomach. Make it black."

"You can take pills for that." I filled the other mugs.

"I take eighty vitamins a day now. I got to piss sometime."

"Just let me know when you two finish fucking so we can talk," Watson said.

"Sorry, Wilson," I said. "I forgot you were there. You want a cruller?"

"Don't want no cruller, no bear claw, no fucking Krispy Kremes. Call me Wilson again, Elron'll sit on your head till it pops. You and I ain't that close."

"Sorry again. I keep forgetting which one goes first."

"Neither one. My first name's Woodrow, but you don't call me that neither. You want to talk or just go on farting through your mouth?"

"So talk." I took a long slug. The caffeine rolled up its sleeves and went to work.

"Sit down first. When I talk to somebody I look them in the eye."

There were several directions I could go with that, but it was too early in the day to have my head sat on by Elron. I slid onto the bench opposite Watson. He sat hunched over the narrow table with both hands around his mug as if to warm them. I seemed to be the only one in the room who sweated.

"How's the labor business?"

"Fuck you care? You belong to a local?"

"No. The detective trade is strictly right-to-work, when you can get it. I was just filling an embarrassing lull in the conversation."

Elron chuckled. He sounded a little like Michael Jackson. I wondered if it was the vitamins.

"Deirdre Fuller," Watson said.

I almost spilled my coffee. It came out "Dee-dee" the way he said it; Darius's pet name for his daughter. But some people had trouble pronouncing it right. I set the mug down carefully. "She's dead."

"She was dead last night on Channel Four. She was still dead this morning on

CNN. I don't read the papers, but I bet you the short money she's dead there too. What I want to talk about is why you think I give a shit."

"I wasn't sure, until you showed up here. If you didn't, you'd be out picketing some gambling hell."

"I ain't got the legs for it. I do give a shit, as it happens, strictly as a fan of her old man's. It wasn't for the sixty-eight Series, I'd of hung myself in my cell. It was my one bright light. I was in a bad way that year. The Man took me down for exercising my civil rights."

"You torched a Radio Shack with the owner lying inside with a concussion you gave him. Cops checked him into Receiving with third-degree burns over sixty percent of his body. I didn't see anything about that in the Constitution."

"That was his choice. No one made him be there, sitting on his merch with a baseball bat across his lap. He was lucky I only hit him with it once. Lots of folks died of dumb that week."

"It was going around," Elron said.

"Shut the fuck up. You wasn't even a stain on your daddy's underpants when all that came down."

"The owner was black," I said. "But I

guess some people's rights aren't as civil as others'."

Watson uncurled a hand from his mug to make an expansive gesture. He had a mermaid tattooed on the heel of his palm. "Over and done and dead. I let go of my anger when my parole came through. They had a honey of a shrink at Jackson. He put me in touch with my emotions. They flew right out between the bars. You read Jung?"

"Young who?"

"Carl Jung, you ignorant son of a bitch. Freud was a dirty old Kraut. When he was running around telling everybody they was motherfuckers, Jung was busy discovering the collective unconscious. We all part of the whole, starting with the monkeys."

"I thought that was Darwin."

"He was an anthropologist. I read everything Jung wrote I could get through the prison library system. I started my own outside. You want to guess how many books been written just about him?"

"Don't," Elron said. "Wilson's got a warehouse full in Sterling Heights. Costs him fifteen hundred a month just for storage."

I said, "You should hang out a shingle. Most cons who read inside come out lawyers. A jailhouse psychiatrist could write his own ticket in this town."

"Deirdre Fuller," Watson said. "Think I had anything to do with that deal?"

"Which deal, the killing deal or the deal you had with Hilary Bairn?"

"He tell you about that?"

I took another pull from my mug. I felt my nerves tamping down. "I know he stumbled into your ATM trap. You sent your boy Esmerelda to talk to him, probably with his famous black toolbox for a visual aid, and Bairn told him about his relationship with Deirdre and the trust fund she had coming. You didn't believe him, or thought two months was too long, long enough anyway for Bairn to figure a way to cheat you out of whatever cut he offered you. Maybe Esmerelda opened his box, maybe he didn't, but whatever he did spooked Bairn into trying to raise cash in a hurry to keep him from driving a nail through his hand.

"Our incarceration system failed you," I went on. "Another year or so of therapy and you might've developed patience. All you did was blow both your chances at a piece of a couple of million. When Deirdre found out he was using her as a fence, she broke off the engagement. They fought, she's dead, and Bairn's got worse problems with the law than he had with you."

"Bairn tell you I turned him down?"

"I never got close enough to ask. He was the job, not the client."

"Know where he is?"

I shook my head. "Neither do the cops. That's what makes him their star."

Watson took his first drink. He blinked both eyes and pushed the mug away. "Strong shit. No wonder you dream funny. Okay."

"Okay what?"

"Okay, I found out what I came here to find out. I got new business with Bairn now his meal ticket's getting sliced up downtown. He offered me ten percent of the two million when it came through. He started out lower, but I had Ernesto negotiate and we reached what they call accord. You're still working if you want to know who's still squeezing him. It ain't me."

"You wouldn't lie."

"What's the point of bluffing when I got Elron in my hand?"

The big man emptied his mug in a jerk and plocked it down on the table. It looked like a demitasse in his paw. "Jesus. Why'n't you just chew the grounds?"

"We got a rally to attend." Watson slid to the end of his bench, spread his feet, and pushed himself upright. "You should consider joining the rank and file. No one should live like this." He swiveled his yellow eyes toward Elron.

The big man curled four fingers around the back edge of the refrigerator, took in a deep breath that swelled his face and turned it red, and pulled. The refrigerator tipped forward in one smooth motion and shook the house when it struck the linoleum.

Elron seemed to notice then he was still holding the scrap of paper in his other hand with my address on it. He looked around as if for a wastebasket, then took a step and laid it gently on the table. He followed Watson out through the living room while I sat and finished my coffee.

TWELVE

"Hey, man."

Fuller sounded a little less worn. Whatever he'd smoked the night before must have given him some rest in spite of the hard floor against his old bones.

I said, "I got a busy signal before. Does this mean you're through making your calls?"

"They got self-help manuals for everything else. They ought to write one for dealing with funeral directors. How big's your trunk?"

"Why, did you kill one?"

"No, I'm moving today. I don't need much space to pack what the buzzards left me. How's my credit with you?"

"Based on the advance you paid, I could move you to South America. What hotel did you pick?"

"That's the thing. Just when you think you know someone you divorced, she turns out human. I called Gloria first thing this morning. We cried a lot, then she offered me the vacation house I gave her in the settlement till I can find a place of my own. She ain't used it in years. Dee-dee went there sometimes," he said after a moment.

"Sure you're up to that?"

"I figure I should get it all out right at the start. Then maybe it won't be so hard later. What do you think?"

"I think it'll be hard regardless. Where's the house?" If it was Detroit Beach I was going to back out.

"Black Squirrel Lake. Know it?"

"If it's got *lake* on the end I'm shaky. Got directions?"

"I can drive it in the dark. We practically lived up there from postseason till spring training."

"I'll bring my rod and reel."

"Hope you like pike. They ate everything else."

I spent a little while getting my refrigerator back on its feet, then opened it to survey the damage. The lightbulb was broken and I'd lost four eggs and a six-pack of Stroh's, but the compressor was still working. There's something to be said for living the spare life of the bachelor. I mopped up the mess and climbed into the traces.

At Alter Street, where Jefferson Avenue stops and Lake Shore Drive begins, a derelict sat on the southeast corner surrounded by his shabby duffels and knotted Wal-Mart sacks, smoking a cigarette and watching a Micronesian gardener edging blue-gray sod on the northwest corner. The derelict belonged to Detroit, the gardener to the first of the private estates that grew progressively larger as the river slowed down and spread to form Lake St. Clair. Which was the dream and which was the reality depended on which way you were driving. When it came to situations, you couldn't come up with a better name for a street in that particular spot than *alter*.

I drove past two miles of scrollwork, topiary, and fleets of stretches and two-seaters, then turned into the white-powder drive between the two gray stone pillars and the rectangles of lawn that looked naked now without furniture, the grass trampled flat and shiny by hundreds of pairs of feet. Arcs of water erupted from underground sprinklers and drifted in apparently aimless patterns, making rainbows in the sunlight hammering down from above. Fuller caught me watching them with my hands in my pockets when he opened the door.

"Somebody forgot to call the water company," he greeted. "I'm running up the bill for Washington. Give me a hand with these, okay? I ran out the warranty in my arm thirty years ago."

He was holding a silver garment bag, a two-suiter, over one shoulder and had a Detroit Tigers duffel at his feet, Domino's blue from the early days of the succession of pizza franchises that had owned the team. I leaned across the threshold and hoisted the duffel by its handle. Behind him the morning sun painted shimmering stripes on a polished walnut floor that swept uninterrupted to the walls. "Looks like they even sold the dust bunnies," I said.

"They went last. Careful with that bag. I'm heading out with a year's supply of lightbulbs."

The duffel wasn't heavy. "Anything else?"

"I thought about faucet handles, but I figured they'd come after me for those."

"I meant personal possessions."

He grinned, reached inside the slash pocket of the team Windbreaker he wore over his sweats, tossed a baseball up above his head, caught it without looking, and returned it to the pocket.

"*The* ball?" I asked.

"That's what the *Sports Illustrated* photographer said when I let Dee-dee play jacks with it. He said I ought to be more careful with a historical artifact." The grin evaporated.

"It looks like she didn't feel anything. For whatever that's worth."

He nodded, but he didn't appear to be listening. He didn't look rangy today, but frail, and every bit of sixty. The gray eyes lacked luster in a face as weatherchecked as an old tire. His gaze drifted out over the lawn. "You missed the TV crews. I hid upstairs and called my lawyer, who's got plants at the stations. Appears I left for California last night."

"That's going to cost."

"When you don't have it to pay you don't worry about it."

I took the envelope out of my breast pocket and stuck it at him. "I'm pretty sure this wasn't reported. The cops have all the federal company they want these days without inviting more."

"It'll help." He folded it one-handed without looking inside and put it in the same pocket with the no-hitter ball. "They find the son of a bitch?"

"If they did they're not announcing it. I didn't want to call and show too much interest. They think I'm off the case. Am I?"

"We'll talk about it on the way. Is *that* your

ride?" He squinted at the Cutlass in the driveway, its blue paint turning to chalk in the sun.

"Don't let the dings fool you. There isn't a thing about the engine that's legal."

We put his bags in the trunk and I slammed the lid. He started to get in on the passenger's side in front, then withdrew his foot and walked down the driveway toward the street. About thirty yards from the house he turned around and stood looking at it for a full minute. Then he took the baseball out of his pocket and flipped it back and forth between his hands. A caterpillar climbed my spine in high heels.

He nodded, a short jerk of his chin, as if approving a signal from the catcher. He clasped the ball in both hands against his chest, then wound up, raising it above his head and lifting his left foot as high as his belt. His right arm swept down and around twice, then back, paused, and snapped out straight as he came down on the foot, lifting the other, putting his whole body into the pitch. The ball vanished from his hand. I heard a whoosh and then a pane jumped out of one of the mullioned windows to the right of the front door with a tinny tinkle.

I was behind the wheel when he came back up the driveway and slid in beside me.

"Sure you wanted to do that?"

"It was like I was carrying around a anvil in my pocket."

"We could go in and get it."

He looked at me. "Now, what'd that do besides take all the point out of the stupidest thing I ever done?"

I didn't have any argument for that. I'd never seen a more convincing suicide note.

I hadn't been through that part of Oakland County in some time. Judging by the housing developments that had sprung up since then, it might have been forty years. We drove past sprawling villages of mammoth houses surrounded by baby shrubs, raw sections of upturned earth dotted with dozers and portable toilets and buildings in every stage of construction, and school after school with temporary classrooms towed in and propped up on blocks to handle the sudden overload. It was one big tribute to Tyvek. I braked twice to avoid colliding with deer looking for a new place to live.

Fuller broke the long silence. "How they figure to feed all these folks when the last farm's plowed under?"

"Plant wheat in the empty cities." A billboard rolled past calling our attention to the future site of yet another Fox Run.

Black Squirrel Lake made a figure eight on the eastern edge of Dodge Brothers State Park, girdled in the middle by a tangle of reeds and pussy willows with a channel running through it. We passed a tiny rustic settlement flanked by a bar and diner, turned at a sign obliterated by buckshot, and followed a gravel track ending abruptly in front of a rectangular house sided in redwood with a front porch running its length. Shaggy plants grew out of copper pots suspended from the roof. "Somebody's going to have to water 'em," said Fuller.

We got out. At around 1100 square feet it was one of the larger houses in its immediate neighborhood. Older tile-and-tar-paper shacks flanked it on narrow lots. A cedar lodge the size of the governor's mansion took up several acres directly across the lake, with a deck overhanging the water and below it a pontoon boat tied to a private dock. Its nearest neighbors were a Cape Cod nearly as large and a Frank Lloyd Wright affair of gaunt girders and glass sheets. That seemed to be the more fashionable side of the lake.

"Come take a look at this."

Fuller had gotten onto the porch to fish the key out of one of the hanging plants. The tone of his voice brought me back up

142

the worn path in the grass I'd wandered down for a closer look at the lives of people who took vacations. He stood with his back to the driveway, the silver garment bag hanging from his hand to the boards. As I stepped up beside him he withdrew his index finger from a neat round hole in the front door, a third of the way down from the top and an inch right of center.

"Squirrel?" he asked.

"Squirrel," I said. "If someone shot it from a gun."

"There's no hunting here. The lake owners' association has its own security."

"Not many people hunt from inside a house. This bullet was traveling our way." I pointed to a bristle of splinters pointing out.

"What the hell." He aimed the key at the lock.

I grasped his wrist before he could turn it. "Those splinters are fresh."

He got it. He let the bag slide the rest of the way to the boards and we backed off the porch.

On the ground I pointed to a corner of the house out of direct view from the windows and he took up that position while I opened the door on the passenger's side of the car and released the spring that opened the little hatch under the glove compartment. The Luger came free of the metal clips with a twist. I checked the magazine, heeled it back into the handle, chambered a round, and circled the house on foot with the barrel raised, seeing what I could of the inside through the windows from ground level. It was useless unless the shooter was careless enough not to stay away from them, but it beat charging the place without a plan. When I got to where Fuller was waiting, I got the key from him and told him to stay put a little longer. Then I crept back up the steps to the porch.

I turned the knob slowly until it stopped. The door was locked. I slid in the key without scraping the sides and turned it just as slowly until the dead bolt slid back with a snap. Then I tightened my grip on the pistol and went in.

No one shot at me, not in the open floor plan of the kitchen and dining and living room areas or in either of the two bedrooms, one larger than the other, or the bathroom that was just big enough for a sink, shower stall, and toilet. The place was tidy, with a piny smell throughout and personal items here and there I didn't bother to stop and study. There was no telephone or television, no video games, just a few paperbacks and a stack of board games in ratty cardboard boxes stacked in a closet to distract the occupants from the entertainments offered by the lake. A genuine getaway spot.

A sliding doorwall let me onto a shallow deck overlooking the water, with an old-fashioned wooden chaise longue, a green resin chair, and a white wicker love seat, where one could sit on the faded cushions, sipping a drink and smacking mosquitoes and watching speedboats razz about and the pontoon boat from the wilderness mansion across the way cruise in circles, leaking dance music and the clink of cocktails being stirred. I poked the Luger under my waistband and leaned on the railing. That gave me a fresh angle on the near shore, and a look at the boxy rear end of an orange Aztek sticking up out of the water.

THIRTEEN

When we got down there, I pointed out the twin tracks where the Aztek's tires had flattened the grass from where it had been pushed or driven off the driveway down to the shore. I'd walked right across them on my patrol around the house, but they weren't obvious and I hadn't been looking at the ground. Where the grass ended and the earth sloped to the water's edge, two furrows led through the mud to the lake. The vehicle had rolled a few yards into the water and hung up with its front two-thirds submerged and the hatch pointed skyward at a thirty-degree angle. I took out my pistol and offered Fuller the butt. "Know how to use one?"

"I grew up on Erskine. Wasn't for baseball I'd probably be doing my time in Jackson. What you want me to shoot?" He took it.

"Whatever moves when I open the hatch." I'd left my coat in the Cutlass. I sat down on the grass, took off my shoes and socks, and rolled my pants above my knees. It didn't make me feel a bit like Huckleberry Finn.

"What's the odds something will?"

"Zero."

"Then what's the point?"

"My arithmetic's not that good."

"Is it Bairn's? There's plenty of these around."

"Not with his plate."

"So this is where he's been hiding. He must've spent some time out here with Dee-dee."

It was another hot day and the water was only a few degrees cooler, but it chilled me like a blast of liquid oxygen when I waded in. The bottom was mucky and oozed between my toes; I might have been walking on a bed of earthworms.

Despite the precautions I was soaked to the waist when I reached the car. I cupped my hands around my eyes and leaned against the back window, but the glass was tinted and I saw only shadows. Nothing seemed to be moving around inside. I reached down for the handle. If the hatch was locked I'd have to go back and leave it for the cops. I should have left it for them anyway, but my judgment's not often better than my arithmetic.

It wasn't locked. The latch clunked when I lifted the handle. I raised the hatch until the hydraulics took over, then got out of the way of anything that might come at me from inside.

Nothing did. I hadn't expected it to, but I'd been shot once for my expectations.

There was plenty of cargo space behind the rear seat, which folded down when extra was needed. It wasn't. The man who lay there with his knees tucked into his chest looked to be only average height and underweight for that. It gave his cheeks that hollow starved look you see in cologne advertisements; his cocoa-brown suit, creased and wrinkled now, would have hung handsomely on his delicate frame. The face was Latin, the disarranged hair thick and black and growing far down on the forehead, the beard blue beneath the skin, lashes long and curling where the eyes stared through them at nothing. He'd bled a little from the hole in his shirt, leaving an oblong patch on the carpeted deck like rusty water stain.

"Who is it, Bairn?" Fuller had a good view from shore.

"No."

Tucked behind the bent knees like an afterthought was a black enamel toolbox the size of a small tackle. I turned up the hinged latch with a knuckle and tipped back the lid. Inside was a stainless-steel hammer with a black neoprene grip and a box of three-inch spikes.

I felt a foolish little pang of disappointment. I'd psyched myself up for a different sort of introduction to Ernesto Esmerelda, Wilson Watson's chief enforcer. It was like cramming all night for an exam, only to find out in the morning it had been canceled.

While we were waiting for a response to our 911 call, Fuller gave me a towel from the linen closet in the house to sponge off the muck and a pair of sweats from his duffel to wear while my trousers hung to dry over the railing of the deck. They were too long for me and I bunched them up around my ankles while my feet appreciated the dry warmth of a pair of white gym socks. We sat on the deck, which bore no visible evidence of Deirdre's occupancy. He'd been sitting less than two minutes when he sprang up, muttering something, and went back inside. I watched a fisherman in an aluminum boat trying his luck among the reeds. My mood brightened when Fuller came back with a bottle of Polish vodka and two barrel glasses pinched between the fingers of one hand.

"Private stash," he said, pouring. "It's been aging all this time under a couple of loose floorboards. I had a leetle problem when I had my slump."

We touched glasses and I drank. The pure grain alcohol scorched my throat going down and vibrated the molecules in the floor of my stomach, producing heat on the microwave principle. "First drink's best, East or West." I'd heard it in an old western.

"First and last," he said. "Everything in between's just something you got to get through."

"Like a slump."

"Hell on earth. Them big bonuses is just an ulcer waiting to bleed. You don't live up to 'em, it's back to the minors. Only they ain't so bad as the worrying about it. Wilson Watson. Seems to me I heard of him."

"He's a gambler," I said. "Also a gangster and a labor leader, which aren't always the same thing. He made a killing on your no-hitter." I'd brought him up to date on the way back from the lake: Charlotte Sing, Hilary Bairn's plunge at Detroit Beach that had put him under Watson's thumb, the stolen watch, Esmerelda's reputation, Watson's visit to my house that morning. I thought laying out the facts might put everything into perspective, but it left me more confused than ever. I took another drink. It was as disappointing as he'd said.

He shuddered. "Gambling, no word's scarier. You can dope or carouse, commit rape, manslaughter, and still get your shot at Cooperstown if you won enough games, but make one call to a bookie and you wind up greeting at Wal-Mart. Look at Pete Rose."

"Showboat."

"Well, then, Denny McLain. First thirty-game winner since Dizzy Dean and the last we'll ever see, but he broke some legs for a gambler and did time, and that's all she wrote. If it'd been for a politician it'd been different."

I let him go on. Sports are always safe. We were up to the World Series That Never Was, a running sore with Fuller, when the fuzz came.

Semifuzz, as it turned out. His name was Fred Loudermilk, and he introduced himself as a captain with security in the service of the Black Squirrel Lake Owners' Association. His Jeep Cherokee was painted sky blue with a lightning-bolt insignia on a white circle on the doors and orange lights clamped to the roof. He wore the lightning-bolt in patches on his sleeves, sky blue also, and a ball cap with the bill bent into a horseshoe curl framing a lean tan face, mirror-finish sunglasses, and a sandy moustache trimmed and trained to follow the curve of the bill. He stood four inches shorter than I on the front porch. "Which one of you placed the call?"

"I did," I said. "I thought I was talking to the sheriff's department."

"We monitor all nine-one-one calls placed from the lake. I'm also an officer in the sheriff's reserve. That means I'm qualified to investigate criminal complaints." He thumbed open a notebook with a spiral on top. "You're Amos Walker, a private investigator? Did you know the victim?"

"Not personally. His name's Esmerelda. He ran errands for Wilson Watson, a semiracketeer in Detroit."

"What's a semiracketeer?"

"A punk who hasn't been caught yet."

He didn't look up from the notebook. "Says here he was killed on the premises. What makes you think so?"

"You're standing on the spot."

He stepped back, lifting his glasses for the first time to stare down at the porch. Neither Fuller nor I had noticed the rusty smear until we'd come back for a second look.

"Bullet came from inside," I said. "There's the hole. He didn't even give him a chance

to knock."

"You're Darius Fuller, a retired b
What's your connection?"

"I built the place. I'm using it or
wife's invitation."

"Call sheet at the office says a l
Fuller is the primary resident. That y
wife?"

"Daughter. She's dead."

Captain Loudermilk knew that. "I'm
for your loss. May I see the victim?"

We took him around back. He went a
as the water's edge, getting mud on
glossy black elastic-sided boots and sati
ing himself with the view through the
tek's open hatch. He asked about the ve
cle's owner and we gave him that part
the story too, but he already seemed famili
with most of it. He was a recording cop.

"It's easy enough to work out," he sai
"Shooter got him from ambush, stowed hi
in back of the SUV, drove it up to the dro
put it in neutral, and got out and pushed
over the edge, counting on it rolling all tl
way into the lake. Either he didn't har
around to see it get stuck or fled when
did. No telling how long it would've gor
undiscovered if it hadn't. These are priva
lots."

He was still speculating when a sheriff

uiser came our way across the grass, fol-
wing the tracks left by the Aztek. It
opped short of the drop. The door came
en on the passenger's side and Inspector
hn Alderdyce got out.

FOURTEEN

"What'd you use, a helicopter?" I asked.

Alderdyce shook his bucket-loader head. He wore gray gabardine with a dusty pink stripe and a pink shirt. He looked as effeminate as a Chevrolet short block. "I can straighten out the surface roads when I get a call that interests me. But I can't hold a match to these county boys, so I left the city car this side of the line and hitched a ride."

That was all the conversation we had for a while. He went over to join the conference with Loudermilk and the sheriff's lieutenant who'd driven the cruiser, a redhead on a heavy frame with a face like a bruised apple, patched all over with heat rash. The lieutenant spent most of his time listening, which was uncommon when dealing with private security. A few minutes later the morgue wagon came, discreetly camouflaged as an overlong station wagon painted slate gray, then the forensics team, and deputies who put on rubber waders and helped the morgue crew haul the body to shore on a stretcher, holding it clear of the water. A tow-truck team parked out of the way while the detail squad took pictures of treadmarks and looked for footprints and broken pen points, then backed the truck around and one of them waded out and found a place for the hook on the Aztek's frame. The winch clanked. In a few minutes Hilary Bairn's ride sat on shore, galled with primordial muck to its rear axle and streaming green slime from the top of its windshield. The sheet metal appeared undamaged.

By this time spectators had gathered, made up of Darius Fuller's neighbors in shorts and T-shirts, drawn by the unusual activity. No one came out of the small shack on the closest lot, with a galvanized roof and swatches of tar paper showing where tile had been stripped off for replacement; a scaffold stood in front and stacks of composition siding lay on wooden pallets next to the driveway, and I noticed for the first time a FOR RENT sign and the name of a realty firm stuck in the lawn. It was the beginning of the gentrification of that side of the lake, only a generation removed from tacky wigwams and bide-a-wee lodges with outhouses in back. Under normal circumstances, protecting the building materials from theft would be Loudermilk's biggest responsibility.

We reconvened — Alderdyce, the security man, the sheriff's lieutenant, and I — in the living room area of the lake house, a cheerful arrangement of rattan chairs and a sofa upholstered with a palm-leaf print, that felt like the waiting room in a funeral home: Fuller's mood, dampened by the recent presence in the house of Deirdre, was contagious. Streaks left by the spray powder the fingerprinters had used contributed to the cloud of gloom. The lieutenant, whose name was Phillips, had made arrangements with Alderdyce to match them with Bairn's prints on file from his apartment.

"Wilson Watson," Alderdyce said, seated on the sofa in a crouch, scraping his palms between his knees. "His name didn't come up last night."

I said, "It didn't seem to matter then. You already figured Bairn was in trouble with the sharks and casinos around. *Who* didn't really matter, if he was desperate enough to blow his shot at two million just to keep the dogs from snapping at his heels."

"You don't get to choose what matters. If

you *had* that privilege, you lost it when Bairn put a bullet in Watson's boy Esmerelda. I could've put a tail on him and we'd have Bairn in custody instead of sending another local thug on his way to cold storage."

"If it *was* Bairn," I said.

"Not much of a jump. He knows by now we're looking for his car, and he had to get rid of the body anyway. It was just his sore luck it didn't sink. His streak's been holding for a long time now." Alderdyce looked at Fuller. "Did you keep a gun here?"

"This is the first time I've been here in twenty years. I gave Dee-dee a pistol when she got a place of her own, a nine-millimeter. It's registered in my name."

"It'd take a nine-millimeter minimum to punch through that door and still be lethal." Loudermilk untucked his necktie from his uniform shirt and used the end to polish his sunglasses. His eyes were blue and protruberant, like pop rivets. "Unlucky or not, he did okay for an amateur. One bullet straight through the pump, with a door between. You'd think he planned it."

Alderdyce looked at me. "You still carrying around that Luger?"

I'd gotten it back from Fuller and put it back in the car. I went out and brought it back. The inspector checked the load and sniffed the barrel. "Everytime I take this from you I think I shouldn't give it back. You ever get around to registering it?" He stuck the butt my way.

"I left the legal piece back in town." I slid it under the elastic of my borrowed sweats.

"Who says it wasn't planned?" Phillips dabbed a folded handkerchief to the scabby red patches on his face and examined the results on the fabric. "This Esmerelda had his toolbox with him. He must've thought he had an appointment."

"Someone else might have tipped him Bairn was here," I said. "Everything Bairn's done up to this point is reaction to something someone else did. You can't lay a trap for a pro like Esmerelda without experience, beginner's luck or no."

"Where'd Watson say Bairn got cash from one of his ATMs?" Alderdyce asked me.

"He didn't."

"Guess."

"Not in front of the law. That half-assed I'm not."

He watched me, putting two fingers to his lips in a gesture made meaningless by the fact there wasn't a cigarette between them. It isn't nicotine that brings people back to their bad habits so much as all the silly leftover movements without a prop.

Phillips said, "Question is, if it's Watson that Bairn was hiding from, who killed Mr. Fuller's daughter?"

Fuller said, "He killed her all right. When she told him to walk, took away the jackpot he was counting on, he struck out like the scared skunk he is and ran." He'd moved on to the anger stage.

"Brings us back to him laying a trap," Loudermilk said. "How'd Watson find out otherwise?"

"Maybe Walker told him." The lieutenant resumed treating his rash. Up close it didn't look transient enough to have been caused by heat and chafe. It was some kind of eczema or psoriasis.

"It wouldn't much matter if I did," I said. "When Deirdre wound up dead all over the news, he knew he wasn't going to get a penny out of Bairn, so he sent his chief crucifixionist to make an example."

Loudermilk wiped the legs of his glasses. "I don't think that's a word."

I looked at him. I wondered what his story was. Most rented heat would have been sent on its way by this time.

Alderdyce went back to scraping his palms. They sounded like two sanding blocks. "Time of death will tell us whether

Esmerelda had time to come looking for him after the story broke. You've got a good coroner's office in this county," he told Phillips.

"We ought to. We got the biggest tax base in the state and half as many murders as Detroit. Bairn can't get far on foot," he added. "His picture's faxed to every unit a hundred miles around."

Loudermilk looked at his watch, put on his sunglasses, said he had rounds to make, and shook hands all around. After he left I told the lieutenant, "You were pretty patient with him."

"He had my job before the administration changed. It doesn't do to get too close to the sheriff when the next election might turn him out of office."

"You don't look worried."

He smiled. "I'm thinking of running myself next time. I've been married to the same woman for twenty-seven years and I don't sleep with the help."

We went outside, where the forensics team was packing up. The morgue wagon had gone and the crowd of onlookers was smaller. They'd begun to return to their cabins to resume their vacations. The smell of grilling meat reminded me I hadn't eaten all day.

"You going to be in your office later?" Alderdyce asked.

"After I catch a bite."

"Make it hearty. This time you're going to tell me everything you did and everyone you talked to since you took this job and everything they said."

"Most of it won't do you any more good than it did me. It's full of dead ends and feathers."

"And you're full of shit."

I went to the edge of the lake and smoked a cigarette while he and the lieutenant were talking to the lab crew. Phillips was going to have a hard time getting into office with that face.

My fisherman was nowhere in sight. Something, a pike or a snapping turtle, poked its head above the surface near the middle of the open water and disappeared. I watched the ripples it made until they, too, vanished in the reeds. I wished I hadn't been kidding about bringing a rod and reel. It would have been nice to stand there making casts while I waited for my pants to finish drying on the deck. The point of the practice wasn't to catch anything, necessarily. It would have been a nice change.

Darius Fuller came down to join me.

"You don't have to wait," he said. "The

inspector offered me a ride to a hotel. I can't stay here."

"He wants to question you some more."

"He would anyway. Maybe this way I get let alone quicker."

"We're finished, then."

He took out the envelope, counted out some bills, and stuck them at me. "I'll come around to your office for the ring."

I took a thousand. "Keep the other five hundred. I only worked two days."

He put away the extra bills and offered his hand.

I took it. "I'm sorry again."

"Not as sorry as the sorry son of a bitch that killed my girl. I hope the cops here don't catch him. I hope he runs to Texas or Oklahoma and kills somebody there, not somebody's daughter, just some no-account, and they slip him the needle. I'll pay forty-nine thousand for a seat in the dugout."

When he left I snapped my cigarette stub out over the water. It had barely touched the surface when something — my pike or my snapping turtle — struck at it. The ripples it made were just enough to set bobbing a little motorboat tied to a dilapidated pier behind the empty shack next door, its outboard tilted forward and covered with brown canvas. I turned toward the road, and as I did I saw the checked curtains in a near window, tucked around the edges of the frame and sill the way people do when they aren't coming back for a while and don't want anyone snooping inside. One of the panels moved just a little.

A strip of shingle-sided buildings stood a couple of hundred yards up the road, just far enough back for customers to park and buy tackle from the hardware store and fresh fish from the market to take home when they bombed out on the lake. For the rest there was the Wooden Duck Bar, a windowless dive, and the Chain O' Lakes Diner bookending the little commercial center on the other side. I went in and sat at the counter and ate a ham sandwich and clam chowder from a can. The coffee at least was fresh and I drank three cups. I wasn't in any hurry to get back to the shack. The sheriff's lieutenant had left two deputies and a cruiser in front and they had a clear view of the lake until the sun went down. No one was coming out before then.

I hadn't lied to John Alderdyce when I'd told him I'd be in my office later that day. I hadn't known then the shack next door wasn't empty.

The proprietress, a colorful old party with a cataract patch under her bifocals, took suspicious notice of my pants, wrinkled and still damp. I paid and went out and drove around the lake. About a third of the way around, the road surface improved and the lots got bigger, no stretching your arm out the window to straighten the kinks and punching your neighbor in the ear. The bigger places had carports, decks as big as any of the houses near Fuller's, and fresh asphalt on the boat landings. I spotted three more signs offering places for rent or lease by Peninsular Realty, the same firm that owned the shack I was interested in. It advertised an 800 number and a Web site, www.pleasantpeninsula.com. Just in case anyone was looking I got out in front of a couple of the available properties and knocked on the doors. If anyone answered, I was an interested buyer. No one did, and the doors were locked. No open houses at Peninsular. I figured the company had three or four million tied up in Black Squirrel Lake alone.

When the sun bled over the water I cruised past Fuller's place and the shack, found a space between a brace of battered pickup trucks parked next to the Wooden Duck Bar, and strolled back down the road. My pants chafed my thighs and had shrunk a little. The Luger pressed against my belt like a tumor.

The two deputies were outside the prowl car. One of them sat on the front bumper smoking while his partner emptied his bladder behind a jack pine contorted into a sideshow shape at the end of the driveway near the road. His urine steamed a little. The nights can be chill in that lake country even in summer.

I waited in a patch of shadow. When the light goes and there's no traffic noise, bodies of still water turn into amphitheaters, magnifying a single footstep on loose gravel into an avalanche. I was stuck in that spot as long as they stayed outside the car.

But I had allies.

Something went *twee* in my ear, then stuck a tiny needle into my cheek. I flinched but let it drink its fill and stagger off through the air, full as a tanker and drunk on hemoglobin, the red-blooded American detective kind. When another stung my forehead I reached up and squeezed it between thumb and forefinger, feeling the pop and the wetness of my own blood. There in the reeds they grow them as big as crows, but not as big as in Southeast Asia, and that was never far from my thoughts.

The two men in uniform were only old enough to have read about it in school. If I had to wait much longer I'd be lumped all over, but I didn't think I had that much longer to wait.

From their direction I heard the first wet smack of a palm on the back of a neck, then another and another. It sounded like two Bavarians dancing.

"Son of a *bitch!*" The deputy from the driveway swung open the door on the driver's side and threw himself into the seat. His partner spiked his cigarette into the grass and joined him a moment later. Doors slammed.

I gave it another minute, then stepped away from the road into a gap between the tile-and-tar-paper shack and a redwood fence belonging to a converted mobile home two doors from Darius Fuller's cabin. There I stopped and began a new period of waiting. Out on the lake, the last blush of the sun faded. What light remained lay like bright metal on the water, then began its slide toward the horizon. A bird singing out its boundaries stopped in midmeasure as if a switch had been thrown. Crickets played their kazoos and somewhere in the isthmus of weeds that separated the top half of the figure eight from the bottom a bullfrog gulped. Everything out there was hungry or on the make or both. I was the only thing around without some sort of plan.

When I could no longer distinguish my nails from the tips of my fingers I started toward the lake. Dew clung to the grass with the consistency of mucilage, soaking through my shoes and socks. It was dark as hell. The moon was new, a black hole punched in a spray of stars, and starlight is a poet's conceit. After traveling forty billion miles there was barely enough to illuminate themselves.

But no one is ever in complete darkness where people live. Buttery squares showed among the houses on the far shore, a blue mercury dot atop a tower, a lantern at the end of a dock. My pupils gathered it all in, backlighting trees, structures, the little motorboat lying as still as a toppled idol alongside the Krazy Kat pier behind the shack. I picked my way down the slope that ended at the water, steadying myself with a hand against the pilings, and selected my spot, leaning against the one second to last in the shadow of the warped decking above my head. I folded my arms, crossed my ankles, wanted a cigarette, and took my satisfaction from the craving.

It might have been fifteen minutes, it

might have been five or thirty. I was pretty familiar with the lake's breathing patterns by then, the plops and slaps and occasional startling gasp of some aquatic mammal coming up for air between dives, a woodchuck or a muskrat, and the new sound was nothing like any of those. It was a long drawn-out note, a climbing chord; the tension spring of a screen door pulled to its limits when the door opened, three feet above my head. A long time seemed to go by before the door bumped back into its frame, guided gently by a hand to avoid a bang. The Luger was in my hand by then. I didn't remember drawing it.

Boards creaked overhead. A little spill of dirt and sawdust fell onto my shoulder. I smelled mold.

The pier swayed under the movement. At least one of the pilings had rotted through at ground level and swung free, like a peg leg. I shifted my weight onto my heels in case the whole affair decided to collapse on top of me.

Something moved between me and the lake, and as it did so the timbers heeled in that direction, pulled by a sudden change in the balance: a body lowering itself into a boat. Resonant thumps sounded like coconut shells on a hollow plank. The figure let go and the pier righted itself.

When he bent to remove the canvas tarp from the motor, I recognized his clean profile, the chin a little fuzzier than usual, the pale pompadour of hair looking neglected rather than artfully untended. The loop in his left ear glittered.

He'd come prepared. Something sloshed and sharp fumes bit the inside of my nostrils. A cap was unscrewed. Liquid gurgled. I waited until he set down the gasoline can and replaced the cap on the tank. When he grasped the handle of the pull rope to start the motor, I stepped from under the pier with the Luger raised just high enough to catch the light. Hilary Bairn saw the movement in the corner of his eye, straightened, and turned my way, reaching across his body with one hand. I tightened my finger on the trigger, but I didn't fire.

"Drop 'em or I'll drill you both!"

This was a new voice. I turned my head just enough to see the silhouette on the pier above, a figure in a ball cap pointing a handgun down at us across the railing in a two-handed police grip.

I dropped mine. Bairn raised his hands above his shoulders. They were empty.

FIFTEEN

Even in the dark without his sunglasses on, I recognized Fred Loudermilk, the security captain employed by the lake owners' association, by his body language and the curl of his cap. I remembered his service piece was a deep-bellied Ruger with a fisted grip, good at twice the range, especially with elevation on his side.

I spread my hands to show they were empty. "Amos Walker, Captain. I was making a citizen's arrest. Meet Hilary Bairn, your shooter."

"Move on up the bank, away from the gun."

"What about Bairn?"

"Move!" He drew back the hammer.

My skin puckered with a sudden chill. I started up the slope.

"Okay, Bairn," Loudermilk said. "Before I change my mind. No, not that. The other."

There was a brief, puzzled silence, then

the whir of the pull rope.

It hadn't been used in a while, or the motor wasn't primed, because it whirred twice more before compression. The motor coughed, sputtered, and started with a roar. And I knew, as Bairn tipped the propeller overboard and the blades churned the water into foam, that if I took another step or even stayed where I was another second, I was as dead as Ernesto Esmerelda.

I threw myself hard down on my shoulder and rolled.

In the direction of least resistance, down the slope and into the lake. The water was cold and boxed my ears when my head went under, but not before I heard the first report, sending a slug through the air where I'd been standing.

It was a braver act than it sounds, or more accurately a dumber one. It was dark, and I had a better than 50-percent chance of Loudermilk's missing me entirely or not hitting anything vital, against a nearly 100-percent chance of drowning. I can't swim. But a gun will make you forget the odds.

I gulped air just before I hit the water, but it burned my nostrils anyway as I slid down the greasy underwater slope on my belly toward deep water. Something zipped past me, burning a phosphorescent path through the black like a tracer and illuminating the cloud of earth it kicked up when it struck bottom, and I clawed with my hands and feet until the slope fell away and I pushed off into an alien element that figured in all my worst nightmares. My lungs expanded to the bursting point; I let some of the air out in bubbles, executed a somersault in agonizingly slow motion, and stabbed with my feet in the direction I hoped was down. They collided with something solid and I stumbled, but overcame momentum and straightened my knees. My head broke the surface, and when I'd swallowed enough air for it I laughed. The lake was only a little more than five feet deep at that point.

Something smacked the water a yard away from me, an oar or a beaver tail. Then I heard the shot. I filled my lungs again and did a deep knee bend. Back under, I made circular motions with my arms to keep from losing my balance. There was an undertow, probably part of the channel that connected the local chain of lakes, and it pulled at the upper half of my body like a slipstream, trying to snatch me off my feet. If that happened, I might as well have stayed onshore and taken a bullet through the head. I saw myself dragged from the bottom with grapnels, or floating to the surface after three days with a belly full of gas, arms and legs stuck out and bloated, a parade balloon drifting toward a slab at the county seat next to Ernesto Esmerelda's.

When I straightened my legs again, more carefully this time so only my eyes and nose pierced the surface, no shot greeted me. I got my bearings from the huge house directly across from Darius Fuller's and turned slowly, trying not to make a splash or a ripple, toward the shack and the pier Loudermilk was using for a shooting stand. There was light where there hadn't been before: the glaring twin stars of a pair of headlamps on high beam. I figured the two deputies stationed in front of Fuller's place had driven their cruiser across the lawn to investigate the shots from next door. I saw Loudermilk's slender silhouette and one other standing on the pier, the security captain gesturing across the lake. I didn't know what story he was telling, but when another light sprang on, brighter than the others, and scraped its heavy beam over the surface of the water — the cruiser's searchlight, swung by the second deputy — I got ready to go under again.

But the light stopped swinging twenty yards to my left. My ears popped then, and

I heard the puttering of an outboard motor evaporating in the distance. The deputy next to Loudermilk leveled both hands across the pier's railing in a stance I recognized from recent experience, but there was no shot. Hilary Bairn had reached the opposite side of the lake, out of pistol range. I realized then that less than five minutes had passed between the time I rolled down the slope into the water and came up for a second look. It had seemed like I'd been out there half an hour.

Loudermilk's story for the deputies was easy to guess: He'd been shooting at a fugitive from justice making his escape in a stolen motorboat. I was a detail to be dealt with later.

Suddenly he was alone on the pier. An automobile engine whined, reversing for a hasty turn, blue-and-red lights flashed, a siren wound up, a door slammed — the deputy from the pier pulling it shut after the cruiser was in motion. The law was in pursuit. In a little while the lake roads would be crawling with backup.

I was holding my breath as if I were still underwater. I let it out and gulped fresh air. It dragged in my throat and boomed in my ears, covering whatever noise the frogs and crickets made as they took back the wilderness from the interlopers from civilization. I closed my mouth, breathing through my nose, trying not to move or make a sound that would draw attention to where I was crouched to my chin in Black Squirrel Lake, because Fred Loudermilk remained at the end of the pier, leaning motionless against the railing, peering out over the water. I was the crack at the point of pressure that could bring his story down in pieces, and there was nothing now to keep him from patching it up.

I don't know how long I waited. I'd lost all sense of time, also sensation in my limbs. I wondered how cold the water had to be for hypothermia to set in. I'd heard it didn't have as much to do with the actual temperature as with the length of time of exposure. When at long, long last Loudermilk pushed himself away from the railing, hesitated with his gun drawn, then turned and walked back in the direction of the shack where Bairn had been hiding, I had to concentrate all my will into my lower muscles to get them to move, then began the long, long wade back to shore.

SIXTEEN

When the water had receded to my waist I adjusted my course, away from the pier and across the front of Darius Fuller's cabin toward a seawall built of concrete blocks and driftwood to keep the lake from flooding the homely little house on the other side when it rose in the spring. It looked uninhabited. Except in the dead of winter, there's nothing more deserted than a vacation community the week before the weekend of Independence Day. For a few minutes, waterlogged and aching all over from cold and muscles held too long at tension, I sat on the damp earth with my back to the seawall, waiting for my heart to slow to a sprint. Then I got up and climbed the incline toward the road, putting the house between me and Fuller's place. It didn't seem likely that Loudermilk would still be staking it out, but on the other hand I hadn't heard him start up his Jeep and pull away. Then again, I hadn't heard it coming when I set my trap for Bairn, so he might have parked somewhere else and come in on foot. I didn't hold the patent on that.

So apart from the fact that I didn't know why he'd kill me to help Hilary Bairn get away, I didn't know where the security captain was, or what tree he might jump out from behind to finish the job.

A sheriff's cruiser swept down the road, siren off but its spotlight swiveling. I ducked it, a suspicious person dripping wet, and it swept on, dragging a train of dust. Not long after came a chain of civilian cars. The dinner hour was over, the patrons of the Wooden Duck Bar and the Chain O' Lakes Diner were headed home to their families. A few of the cars slowed as they passed Darius Fuller's cabin; the story of the body in the car and the shooting behind the house next door would have spread around the lake by now. That was the difference between country and city. In Detroit, people sped past crime scenes all the time without a second look.

The last vehicle passed and the neighborhood got quiet again. I let it, then started again for the road.

I was passing a tall cedar when something hit the ground with a thump at the base, standing every skin cell I owned on end. I leapt back — and saw something black and glistening and no longer than my foot thump through the grass in the collateral light of a latecoming vehicle accelerating to catch up with the others. Black squirrels are genetic freaks, not really a breed, rarely seen in the Great Lakes and almost never anywhere else, and seeing one is supposed to be good luck; but if they were common enough where I was to have a lake named after them, I wasn't putting any store in it.

I crossed the road without any more incident and turned toward the little commercial strip, barren-looking now with fewer cars in front, with a gap of darkness between the bar and the diner where the daytime businesses had turned out their lights. On the other side of the road, both the cabin and the tar-paper shack remained dark. The deputies hadn't returned from their search for Bairn on the other side of the lake. That was no surprise. Loudermilk had taken just long enough to explain the situation to give him time to beach the motorboat and lose himself in the copses and fields and acres of trailer parks beyond.

Country music, the old-time variety, twanged and thumped through the walls of the Wooden Duck, where the diehards would still be sitting huddled over their bottles and glasses like cavemen protecting their food from one another. Their wired-together pickups and scabrous SUVs were parked in the side lot where I'd left my car. I tore my pocket disentangling the keys from the wet lining and inserted one in the lock.

"Don't move."

This time the command came in a hoarse guttural, but I recognized the voice and saw Fred Loudermilk's reflection in the glass on the driver's side window. The muzzle of his Ruger pointed at the back of my head. He'd remembered my car from before, spotted it in the lot, and waited for me to return to it, around the corner of the building or between parked vehicles.

I froze in a half stoop with the key in my hand. He stepped forward, tickling the nape of my neck with the big revolver while he slipped his free hand under my arms and moved down toward my waist.

"Hey, Fred! What happened out at the Fuller place?"

Hand and weapon came away from me, clothing rustled as the security captain took his gun out of sight and turned to deal with the newcomer from inside the bar. I didn't pause to look at him. I spun around, struck something with my elbow, and followed through, raking the jagged end of the key across the face under the ball cap. The gun went off, glass shattered. I went with my momentum, bodychecking Loudermilk out of my path; then a pair of arms as big around as pilings closed around me from behind and I felt hot breath on my cheek and smelled beer and pork rinds. In every bar there is at least one good samaritan willing to step forward and give local authority a hand. This time he just had to be the first one on the spot.

A pair of hands built for wrapping around glass mugs clamped under my solar plexus and squeezed. I lifted my knee to my chin and slammed my heel down on an instep. The man blew out a fresh blast of fried pig and ferment and broke his grip. I took off running. There was no time to unlock the car and start the motor. My only chance was the lake, always the lake.

The Ruger barked again as I cleared the road. Gravel skittered, a piece stung my ankle. I thought it was a bullet. I kept moving, aiming again for the deep shadow between Fuller's cabin and the shack next door. I didn't know what excuse Loudermilk had given his helpful friend or if he'd tabled that for later. I'd gotten away from him twice, and if I made it this time he would be the one who had to run. You can always think up a plausible story once you've taken out the only witness against it.

On the slope my feet went out from under me and I rolled again, but this time I braked myself with a foot partway down and threw myself sideways, sliding into home plate under the old pier that belonged to the shack, where I'd been standing the first time Loudermilk drew down on me. There I rose into a crouch, breathing too heavily to listen for footsteps closing in, and scraped at the bare earth with my foot, then fell down again on my hands and knees and groped. If I lived through this it would pay to drop a dollar on a key-chain flashlight.

Boards creaked above me. Dirt and saw-dust hissed down from the cracks between. I was back where I'd started.

The creaking stopped. I went motionless, breathing through my nose.

"Come out, Walker."

It was Loudermilk. I leaned my weight back from my knees, raising them a little and supporting myself on my fingertips, a starter's position. My blood roared in my ears.

"Give it up. I won't shoot."

He must have heard something, or made

an educated guess. The Ruger barked. Something chugged into the earth a few feet from the house and a shaggy circle lighter than the black underside of the boards opened between me and the night sky. The pier shuddered from the impact.

"Liar."

It was a whisper, but he had good ears. Two more holes punched through, close enough to kick dirt onto my shoes. I gave up looking for the Luger I'd dropped earlier. It could have slid a long way down that slope, or the security captain might have found it and taken it away. I rose. He fired again, missing me by three inches. I back-pedaled in a panic and struck something hard behind me that flattened my lungs. It yielded slightly; one of the old pilings that supported the pier, rotted almost through at the base. Feet scraped the boards — Loudermilk, scrambling for balance as the structure swayed beneath him. "Mother-*fuck!*"

When you're out of aces, you play the deuce.

I turned my shoulder into the piling, set my feet, and pushed.

The pier was solider than it looked. It swung that way, not enough, and I leapt away from the piling a tenth of a second before a bullet crashed through the boards and whacked it on the side, spraying splinters; something grazed my cheek an inch below the right eye.

Before he could steady his aim for another try I charged the piling, shoving with both hands. It tilted, and half a ton of weathered wood listed thirty degrees and stood still.

Loudermilk didn't. Leather soles skidded on wet slime and he hit the railing with all his weight. On instinct I grasped the piling with both hands and pushed with everything I had left. It gave, then stopped. It was holding on by sheer habit. But I had the strength of two, or at least the weight. Loudermilk's against the railing brought a groan from the pier. It went on groaning like a lovestruck whale, then something cracked with a beautiful splitting peal of surrender and went on over, wrenching nails out of timbers weakened by age and climate and seasons of neglect, showering dirt and crosspieces and old fish scales that twinkled like sequins and a chunk of something hard that struck the top of my left shoulder with a punishing blow. I gasped, but I clambered toward open space, and as I clambered my toe caught something solider than board or timber. I bent and scooped it up on the run. I had a tight grip on the Luger when I dived clear of the tumbling mass of beams and planks and Captain Fred Loudermilk.

SEVENTEEN

Sheriff's substations couldn't exist but for the invention of concrete. Function without form, pipes and cables and circuit boxes exposed, all the nerves and arteries and braids of muscle out there for everyone to see. Polyurethane sealed the slab floor and the furniture had all the permanency of base camp on Everest. The nearest neighbor was a pile of rock salt.

Since there was no place to rest my eyes I closed them, and when they opened to the clearing of a throat that sounded too close to a motorboat starting, I realized I'd been asleep. Lieutenant Phillips sat solid as the building behind a laminate desk heaped with requisitions and curled paperbacks, the raw patches on his big face liverish under the fluorescents. "Rise and shine, lazy-bones," he said. "It's a bright new day."

My gaze drifted toward the only window, square with two crosspieces like a child's drawing. It was set six inches deep and no light came through from outside.

Phillips saw what I saw. "Oh, the sun won't get the memo for a couple of hours. Daylight Savings Time's a bitch on those that have to be at work early."

"Did you ever go home?"

"I went home and ate supper. Tigers had six runs on the Indians when I had to leave."

"How bad did they lose?"

"Tied in the ninth and gave up three in the eleventh. Loudermilk's in Beaumont with a concussion and a broken hand."

"I broke it when he wouldn't let go of the Ruger. Half-unconscious and he still wanted to kill me. What's his story?"

"We'll ask him when he comes around. It's still only your word things weren't the other way around. My deputies almost drilled you when they found you standing over him with that German gun."

"I don't guess they ever caught up with Bairn."

"You don't-guess right. I had them pull Loudermilk's jacket at headquarters. It was full of citations and commendations. One insubordination beef for back-talking the current sheriff, just enough to demote him and force him to quit. I got the head of the lake owners' association out of bed. They were about to renew his contract as captain of security. Two break-ins in four years, and the property was recovered both times. Bit of a jump from there to aiding and abetting a fugitive in two murders."

"I thought so too, and I didn't know his record. But how would I know about Bairn getting away if I weren't there to see it?"

"This is a small community, and everybody tells fish stories. It was all over the lake before I got the call. I'll just hang on to this for now." He picked up my Luger from the desk and put it in a drawer. He must have brought it in with him. "The only permit in that wet mess of a wallet of yours was for a Smith revolver. That's trouble."

"It's spent more time in police custody than in mine. I guess no one wants to do the paperwork. Am I under arrest?"

"I haven't decided yet. I called Inspector Alderdyce, but he said he probably wouldn't see anything my boys hadn't. He said I could house you at County but there wouldn't be any satisfaction in it. Said to tell you you missed an appointment with him at your office."

"I was seduced by the local beauty." I remembered something. "What's Peninsular Realty? It seems to hold title on the whole lake."

He touched one of the rough spots on his face, measuring it between thumb and forefinger. It seemed to be a progressive condition. "Not quite, but they may not be finished. They're out of Benton Harbor. It was all locally owned until a couple of years ago, then the old-timers started dying off and their kids didn't want to mess with fixing up those old shacks; there's not a one of them up to code. I figure the Peninsular people finished buying up Lake Michigan and decided to move inland."

"They're that big?"

"Big enough anyway to drop upwards of three quarters of a million building those two big houses on the north shore and lease them to a GM board member and what-you-call a hip-hop musician in Bloomfield Hills that only use them weekends and vacations. We've been out to the hip-hop place three times already this summer on loud-music complaints and a fight involving a brandished firearm."

"Loudermilk couldn't handle them?"

"They made him a captain, the owners' association did, but he's all the full-time security they have. Couple of moonlighters from the Iroquois Heights Police Department to help out when he needs it, but a private patch doesn't haul much freight with

189

that rap crowd. You're hard put to find one without a felony record. Makes you kind of nostalgic for the days when all they did was trash hotel rooms and punch out the boys from the press." He moved a shoulder. "I know what the association pays Loudermilk, and it ain't enough. If he did go sour, that'd be one good reason."

"You know him better than I do," I said. "All he did was shoot at me a couple of times around the cylinder. You'd know if he was the type. Commendations and citations only cover what goes on in public."

"Personally, I think he's a prick. He's a competent cop, which don't get me wrong, counts for plenty, so when he's got an opinion I listen. But he got as high as he did because he knew when to agree with the old sheriff and just how long to wait before he said no. And *I'm* a political animal, so you can put what I say wherever you want on your scale. If you ask do I think somebody can crook him, I have to say it could happen to anybody, and I never knew a busted cop that wouldn't cut all the corners he had to to get himself reinstated. But I'm just enough of a cop myself not to take the word of a civilian when he squawks about police corruption. That card gets played too much to throw in my hand every time it shows. That answer your question?"

"Not at all. You've got a good chance of being elected."

He chuckled, not entirely without mirth. "All I can say to that is I wish you were registered to vote in this county."

"Who's the local rep for Peninsular Realty?"

"Violet Pershing. She's president of the lake owners' association, the one I got out of bed to vouch for Loudermilk. She lives rent-free in a show home down from the big cedar where the GM guy leases, can't miss the sign. Planning on joining our little community?"

"Don't pretend you didn't dig up my background, Lieutenant. We both know I couldn't afford the shack with the busted pier."

"Destruction of private property, that's something else I can hit you with if I feel like it. Not that it wasn't coming down anyway along with the house when Peninsular takes over. I don't know what you expect to get out of Mrs. Pershing. She's a looker, and they're born on the defensive. Anyway I don't see how the company figures."

"Chances are it doesn't. Most of my hunches pop up into the catcher's mitt. But if it's the biggest landowner on the lake, it's got deep enough pockets to buy a whole fleet of security captains."

"Which brings us to why. I thought Fuller fired you."

"He let me go because the job went away when his daughter was killed. Now I'm under hack with Oakland County *and* the City of Detroit. Maybe I can turn something, buy a little goodwill. It's worked in the past. That is, unless you've made up your mind to house me. What are they serving tomorrow night? In Detroit it's franks and kraut."

"Spaghetti, I think, but you don't get a taste. I'm kicking you on Alderdyce's recommendation. According to him you're a pain in the ass with principles. I guess you bought a little goodwill at that."

"Thanks. What about my pistol?"

"Oh, I don't mind a little paperwork if it keeps one more illegal piece off the streets. I'm a tad weak with the gun-control demographic."

"I'll miss it. My father brought it back with him from Berlin."

"Philippines, mine. All he brought back was himself, and he left a leg on Guam."

"The greatest generation."

"He went to prison for killing a man in a bar fight."

"That why you became a cop?"

"No, it was just a job till I found something that suited me."

"Still looking?"

"Gave up. I'm a bitter, disappointed man, Mr. Walker. Don't fuck up my investigation."

The diner opened at dawn, for fishermen and vacationers who wanted to get an early start on the antiques malls and what-not shops up-country. One of the deputies from the Fuller detail had driven my car to the substation when his partner took me in for questioning, and I'd stopped at a twenty-four-hour gas station and convenience store for cigarettes to replace my sodden pack. Waiting in front of the Chain O' Lakes I'd smoked three or four, scratching my unshaven neck and trying to find a position on the front seat where my damp clothes didn't chafe the skin. The woman with the eye patch liked what she saw even less than she had the day before, so I made quick work of the eggs and bacon and didn't finish my second cup of coffee. That made it still too early to go calling. I drove three miles to a Wal-Mart, bought a package of disposable razors, a can of Barbasol, and a complete change of clothes down to a pair of sneakers, and shaved and changed in the rest-room, leaving the wet rags and cracked shoes behind in the trash basket. Without a client to go expenses, the cost of a new suit to replace the old was going to have to come out of the general operating budget. Except I'd gone over that on breakfast.

I still needed sleep, but the makeover made me feel better about the prospect of dropping in on a stranger unannounced. The house was one of those I'd stopped at after Fuller and I had parted company and found no one home, a Cape Cod modest by the standards of that neighborhood, but with a smart coat of white paint, enameled black shutters, and on each side of the driveway an anchor set in concrete, big enough to sink any boat capable of navigating the shallow waters. The Peninsular sign on the lawn advertised it as a model home. A weather vane shaped like a sextant straddled the roof and there was a porthole in the door. The doorbell buzzed, a disappointment. I'd expected it to play "Barnacle Bill."

"Goodness, you're early."

"Am I?" I smiled at the woman who'd answered, a small brunette built to scale in a blue silk blouse, white ducks, and dock-siders, artfully scuffed at the toes. Her hair spilled blue-black to her shoulders and she had a long straight nose, good chin, and elongated eyes like you see in Egyptian hieroglyphs. She was in her late twenties.

"I didn't expect you before nine."

"I didn't expect you to expect me anytime. My name's Walker." I showed her the ID, rescued from its soaked folder and baked in the sun on the dashboard. The printing was blurred but the picture still looked like me.

"I'm showing someone the house later," she said. "Is this about the shooting? I didn't see or hear anything. I got in late last night."

"Are you Violet Pershing?"

She smiled. She had nice white teeth, but here was one good-looking woman who knew when to stop the orthodontist. The canines came to points. "I'm younger than you thought. I get that a lot."

"I've never met a woman named Violet under sixty."

"It was the name of my father's sponsor. He remained grateful to her till the day he died."

"Was he in TV or radio?"

A crease marred the smooth cream of her forehead. "Oh! Sponsor. The woman who put up money for his passage after Saigon fell and set him up in this country. Not all the people who opposed the war sat back smugly after the troops cleared out. If it weren't for her I'd never have been born, or at least I'd be a different person. He met my mother over here."

"Your father was Vietnamese?"

"Laotian."

I poked that into one of the pigeonholes inside my skull. It didn't have to mean anything. "I'm investigating the shooter, not the shooting. May I come in?"

"If you don't mind my removing the breakfast things while we talk. A toast crust and coffee rings can queer a rental."

"I'll help."

"You'll watch. Nothing gets in the way worse than a man trying to make himself useful in a strange kitchen."

I agreed to the terms and followed her through a living room done in smoked glass and putty-colored fabrics into a gleaming kitchen. She cleared a granite counter of a saucer of crumbs, a jadeite mug, and a cut-crystal juice glass, wiped down the top, and placed the items in a dishwasher with a control panel full of twinkling colored lights. When she pressed a panel to turn it on it made no more noise than a goldfish swimming laps in a bowl. I sat at the counter and admired the long firm line of a haunch when she bent to deposit a paper towel in the wastebasket under the sink.

"Does anyone else live here besides you and Mr. Pershing?"

"Mr. Pershing lives in Miami with the Cuban woman who used to clean our house. We're divorced."

"Sorry. About the housemaid, I mean."

"Thank you. I don't date detectives, private or otherwise."

"We have that in common, at least. Lieutenant Phillips with the sheriff's department says you spoke in favor of Fred Loudermilk's character."

"His character never came up. I said he was efficient at his job."

"So you don't like him."

She tore another paper towel off a roll on a marble spindle and wiped down the sink and faucet. "It happens I don't, but I didn't say that. If I hired someone I liked to look after the security of the residents and he wasn't any good at the job, it would mean I'm no good at mine. I don't like men who swagger, but perhaps the way he conducts his responsibilities gives him that right. I thought you said you were investigating that man Bairn."

"That was a different shooting. I'm trying to find out why Loudermilk shot at me."

That stopped the cleaning frenzy. She left the towel on the drain board and turned my way. "I hadn't heard anything about that. You're sure it was Fred?"

"Both times. The second time an ambulance took him to Beaumont Hospital. I had a little help from gravity."

"That doesn't make sense."

"It did to him, but he isn't explaining himself until the doctors patch up the bruise on his brain. Actually, I lied: I know why he shot at me. I'm the only one who can testify in court that he helped a suspect in two homicides escape arrest."

"Hilary Bairn? Impossible. I heard about him on the news. He's nothing more than a desperate fortune hunter. What could he offer Loudermilk to take a risk like that?"

"I hoped you could answer that one. Loudermilk answers to you."

"He answers to the association. The owners elected me to bang the gavel when we meet and to sign checks on the joint account for security and maintenance."

"That's another question I had. Why's it called the lake owners' association when so few of them actually own property on the lake?"

"The name's a holdover from when most of them did. After Peninsular bought them out it didn't seem worth the trouble and expense of having new stationery printed on a technicality. Anyway, 'lake renters' association' doesn't carry the same authority. And there are a few single owners left. Gloria Fuller's one. She owns the house where I understand that man was shot. Her ex-husband is Darius Fuller, the retired baseball player. Ah." She nodded. "You're working for her."

"Him, actually. That's about to become public knowledge if it hasn't already. Right now, though, I'm working for myself. The pay stinks, so I'd like to wrap it up quick. Isn't it rare for a realty firm to deal only in rentals?"

"Not really, and it's going to get less rare as land values increase. There's a lot more money to be made from a long-term lease than a one-time sale. But I'm only an employee, trained to extoll the virtues of life on Black Squirrel Lake. If you want to know how Peninsular works, you'll have to talk to Charlotte Sing."

EIGHTEEN

I blinked. It might have been the glare off all those polished surfaces in eyes gritty from no sleep. "Charlotte Sing is Peninsular Realty?"

"Principal stockholder, anyway. I don't suppose anyone actually owns a big company anymore. That sort of went out with Henry Ford. But she comes close. Not many of the others would vote their shares against her without giving it plenty of thought. That's just a layman's guess," Violet Pershing added. "We've never met."

"I've met her. You got it dead on. I thought she rented only to casinos and massage parlors and sex shops."

"That's her parent company, Pacific Rim Properties. Peninsular's a subsidiary. She learned nothing from the last crash if not diversification. Opinion once again."

"She know you're this candid?"

She got rid of another waterlogged paper

towel and crossed her arms. "I don't kid myself anything I said about her wouldn't get back to her, but I'm not worried. I've closed more deals for the firm than any other agent. She places results above blind loyalty."

"Also you're Asian."

"Half Asian, like her. She has a preference, but it wouldn't mean anything if all I did was sit on my nice tight butt. I saw you looking before," she said. "This whole kitchen is one big mirror."

"I'm a more accomplished lecher usually," I said. "I didn't get my eight hours."

"I don't mind. If I did I wouldn't spend an hour on the treadmill every day. Would you like to see it?"

I didn't have an answer for that right away. I was working at half speed.

"I mean the treadmill. The house has a custom gym, just a sample of how far Peninsular will go to make its tenants feel they're home. You look like a man who stays in shape."

"Don't count on it. Half of my food groups are tobacco and alcohol. Thanks for talking to me, Mrs. Pershing. Any relation to the general?"

"Stuart thought so. He spent his Christmas bonus one year getting a genealogist to connect the dots. What is it with you men and war?"

"Don't ask me. I'm a pacifist as of this morning."

She discovered a stray crumb and flicked it off the sink counter with a neatly rounded nail. "Rain check on that house tour? You don't have to look at the treadmill."

"I thought you didn't date detectives."

"Who said anything about dating?"

I grinned and said I'd bring my sweats.

I needed to surf the Net, starting with pleas-antpeninsula.com, the site listed on Penin-sular's signs. I didn't own a board. Water trickled from my cell phone when I flipped it open; the LED was dark. I spent some change in the same place where I'd bought cigarettes, but Barry Stackpole, my resident Web sleuth, had a message on his machine saying he was away for a week. The machine was new. He wrote about big-time crime, so he might have been anywhere from Phoenix to Foochow. I drove home and set my alarm clock for next year.

Adrenaline had me twisting in the sheets. I got up and opened a bottle of something and brought it back with me to the bed-room. I drank just enough to dull the thud of my heart, put the cap back on, and stretched out spread-eagle in my underwear. Even the crickets were quiet. It was too hot to go looking for a date.

My neighbors' fireworks swam my way through the dark shallow waters of Black Squirrel Lake. That made it night. I was having my old drowning dream, and the reports sounded like gunshots fired from shore, or maybe Wilson Watson's man Esmerelda, hammering nails through someone's hand in hell. At some point the noises got louder and more personal. Someone was knocking.

The room was dark. I figured if I didn't turn on any lights my visitor would go away. He didn't, but I still had hope. I groped my way through the living room without touching any switches and opened the door a crack, holding the first thing I'd thought to grab in lieu of a firearm, the bottle from my nightstand.

It was less than adequate to deal with someone like Mary Ann Thaler, a lieutenant until recently with the Criminal Investigation Division of the Detroit Police Department. She was a handsome woman still and would be for a great many more years, but it took me a second to recognize her without her glasses. She'd had the operation.

"Happy Fourth," she said. "I hope you

didn't think you had to dress."

I realized I was wearing only a pair of shorts, but it was too late to do anything about that. I said, "I thought you were in Washington, learning to be a marshal."

"OJT. I know this jurisdiction." She had one of those voices that sell lots of water beds late at night. "I came to find out what you and Madame Sing had to talk about the other day."

NINETEEN

I put on a robe and slippers and a pot of coffee and sat opposite her in the breakfast nook. She was wearing her light brown hair longer these days and could have exchanged her government-approved grayish pink suit for a sweater and short skirt and infiltrated any high school cheerleading squad in the city.

"What's Justice's interest in Charlotte Sing?" I asked. "I thought your job was to transport prisoners and relocate snitches from L.A. to Squashed Possum, Nebraska."

"It's all been reshuffled so many times since that goddamn September, nobody's quite sure who does what. That's a newbie's take, not to be confused with a statement of federal policy. As to Charlotte Sing, she's been under surveillance for months, and that's as much as I'm cleared to say." She took one sip, said, "Jesus," and spooned a heap of sugar into her cup.

"I like it chunky style." I shook my head. "Not good enough, Lieutenant. Is it still Lieutenant?"

"For two weeks. I gave notice. It won't be Marshal for a while. In order to place you in custody as a material witness, I'll have to call my supervisor."

"Your job's changed, not mine. We've had this conversation before. I'm a natural-born citizen, no wants or warrants or parole restrictions. I go where I want when I want and I don't have to lie about it even to my diary."

"The country's changed, don't forget. Habeas corpus is starting to look like a quaint suggestion. The system's all in a tangle, like I said. You could get snarled up in it for months."

I drank coffee. It still had some bark on it, at that. "You want to make a good impression first time out. I've got a Rolodex full of lawyers and every one of them would give up the beach house in Malibu for a crack at the Supreme Court. You're too small a fish to have something like that in your jacket. They'll cut you into chum and throw you to the sharks."

"So early in the day to start threatening each other. We don't mellow, do we?"

"Maybe it isn't too late to start."

"You first."

I grinned. "Okay. I was working a case for the father of a young woman who wound up dead. Deirdre Fuller."

"I know the history. I kept in touch in case I bombed out in Washington. My father took me to see Darius Fuller pitch once. All I remember is I got mustard on my favorite skirt."

"I bet it was a pinafore. Did you wear mary janes?"

"Yeah, we were guests of Calvin Coolidge. Charlotte Sing," she prompted.

"The suspect in the investigation, which wasn't an investigation then, showed all the signs of a man in deep with the kind of character they coined that phrase for. That suggested gambling, which led me to Madame Sing. It didn't pan out, but she gave me Wilson Watson as a lead. It was a good one, because Watson paid me a personal visit after I tried to make contact. He had coffee too, right where you're sitting. His boy Ernesto Esmerelda took a bullet on his way to visit my suspect at Black Squirrel Lake; that's in Oakland County."

"I know where it is," she said. "I knew it before the story broke last night. One of Sing's companies owns most of the property there."

"I wish you hadn't been out of town. You could've saved me a lot of time and a dip in the lake. Now you go."

She stirred her cup. "Gambling's the least of it where her story's concerned. If it were just that we'd leave it up to the state commissions. I think you know what we're most interested in just now."

"Shoe bombers."

"That's TSA's headache. We're concentrating on how they get in this country to begin with."

"We've got the two longest national boundaries in the world. Start there."

"*That's* INS's headache. We're after the source. The income Madame Sing gets from the casinos and hook joints — through legal channels, no less, rental property with nothing to link her to the operations themselves — is just a stake to finance her smuggling business. She's the single largest importer of illegal immigrants in the country, possibly the world; all the foreign agencies are in the same boat, keel over sail, so we can't be sure of that. Except Israel, and they've got their hands full trying not to become illegal immigrants on their own soil."

"I've been hearing things on the news," I said. "Ordinary folk getting paid a few thousand by strangers to transport Asians across the bridge and through the tunnel. Kind of a reverse Chinese takeout."

Now she smiled. "The P.I. P.I. If I were quoted saying something like that I'd be up before Congress."

"Congress would never know what hit it. Those cases were lunkheaded. Even on short acquaintance I wouldn't tie her to any of them."

"They weren't hers, we're sure of that. The people she uses aren't virgins and they charge the going professional rate. So far we can't link her to card-carrying Islamic extremists, but they've been doing a lot of recruiting among Asians, many of whom share the same views of the Stars and Stripes as their neighbors in the Middle East. She's been working her way up to the top of the food chain, priority-wise."

She was even beginning to sound like a government spook. "She didn't strike me as that type either," I said.

"She isn't. She's an A-number-one capitalist, and those oil-soaked creeps have the deepest pockets on the planet. The poorer you start out, the richer you want to be, and she started out as a slave. The mystery we have to crack before we move in is where she's getting her cash to invest. Gambling doesn't begin to cover what she's laying out.

Did I mention all this is classified?"

"Thanks for the vote of confidence."

"Don't waste your breath. If I thought you could do anything with it I wouldn't be here. I know from years of experience you're a pump that needs priming." She wrapped her upper lip over her cup, then set it down and pushed it away. "I hate sugar. So on the level, this Hilary Bairn character is all you talked about?"

She wasn't letting me off the hook, and I was too tired to wiggle off. "Bairn went bust at Detroit Beach and wound up in hock to Wilson Watson, then went to her to borrow against what he expected to come into when he married the Fuller woman. Anyway, that's what he told her, she said. When she showed him the door he tried to raise money to put off Watson. When that didn't pan out, and his meal ticket died — by his own hand, probably, during a lovers' quarrel — he fled to her mother's place on the lake. Esmerelda tracked him there, with his toolbox; you know about his toolbox?"

"Everyone in Felony Homicide knows about the toolbox. You think Bairn shot him?"

"What I think stopped counting when Darius Fuller took me off the job. A sheriff's lieutenant thinks it, and so does John Alderdyce. Esmerelda's body in Bairn's Aztek gives it some weight. Also I caught Bairn trying to escape from his hidey-hole in the shack next door." I told her what had happened then.

She nodded. "I got all that from John. This security schmoe Loudermilk is government property, if he wakes up. You might have left a little more of him for us to work on."

"I hit him just as hard as I could with the only weapon I had available. He still out?"

"He's conscious, but his doctors are still stiff-arming us. But we've got as many lawyers as they have. I feel bad for John," she said, apropos nothing. "You know they're about to take his job away from him?"

I put down my cup. My brewing skills had deteriorated along with most of the others. "Not for the way he's been handling this investigation. He wrote the book."

"The mayor and the chief can't read. They're getting ready to reorganize the department: layoffs, of course, and they want to consolidate the precincts into districts. The worst part is they're doing away with the rank of inspector. That means promotion to commander, if you're close enough to city hall, but John's been too busy doing his job to line up dates for the annual mayor's convention on Mackinac Island, so he's looking at lieutenant. He won't stand for it, which is what they're counting on, because inspectors are expensive to keep. They'll shove him into early retirement without having to hike his pension."

"He seemed a little thornier than usual. I thought it was the leaky roof downtown."

"That's part of it. It's an old slumlord's trick: let the facilities go to hell and drive out the tenants, then go condo. Why do you think I sent my resumé to Justice?"

"You didn't sound as if you were committed to the job."

"A girl has to keep herself in pantyhose. I tried to convince John to go with me, but he's got a family, and Detroit's in his blood. He said he wouldn't last six months in historic Georgetown."

"He's right. He was born at Henry Ford."

"What else you got besides this radiator flush?"

I got up, dumped out the cups in the sink, came back with two glasses, and poured us each three fingers from the bottle I'd brought from the bedroom. We clinked.

"Isn't this breakfast for you?" she asked.

"Jet lag. Aren't you on duty?"

She fluttered her lips and drank. "That's

not much better. You ought to be able to afford better with your overhead."

"Everything's relative." I finished ahead of her and bought another round. "I'm not the office watercooler. Why bitch to me?"

"This Fuller case is high-profile," she said. "He's almost the only sports hero this town has left. If John can break it and break it big, the chief won't have any choice but to kick him upstairs. Only he can't, because we won't let him. Not if it means jeopardizing the Charlotte Sing investigation."

"Am I going to like where this conversation is headed?"

"If some concerned individual in the private sector should manage to lay his hands on Bairn and turn him over to the Criminal Investigation Division, there isn't a whole hell of a lot Uncle Sam could do to reverse the gears."

I turned that over with gloves on. All my prepared dialogue was based on people in positions of authority telling me to lay off. "Are you hiring me?"

"Not on a government salary. But a thing like that would go a long way to square you with Detroit."

"And screw me with Washington. If I louse up the Sing case and they trace it to you, they'll revoke both our citizenships."

"Nothing that drastic, but we'll probably both be audited. I'll be out of a job, of course, but like the man said, I was looking for a job when I got this one."

"What's your end?"

She clattered a set of clear-polished nails on her glass. "If it weren't for John Alderdyce, I'd still be in the blue bag on Stationary Traffic. The old mayor — you know the one I mean — had the son of a friend all lined up for the vacancy in Felony Homicide. I had the chops, but the son had the testicles. John threatened to bring in the union."

"He went on suspension once. He wouldn't talk about it."

"That was part of the deal to put him back on duty. He hadn't been an inspector long enough to make demands, but the administration was in too bad a cess with the DPOA as it was to piss off the rank-and-file over one more issue. John won, but he knew he'd never make commander as long as anyone remembered what he did. Now I'm in a position to do him the same solid. You, too. He could've busted you down to a job with mall security a dozen times; the licensing board would've listened to him. Twice I tried to get him to do just that. I'm not asking any favor you don't already owe."

I took another hit, but it did nothing to stiffen my spine. I did need a better brand. "What else can you tell me about Charlotte Sing?"

"She's my territory. Bairn's yours."

"They've overlapped twice now. I may have to bag her, too."

Twenty

It was Friday, the first day of the Independence Day weekend. That made for four days of deserted expressways downtown and in the suburbs and choked arteries to the North and West. A truck dumpover at dawn, a chain collision at seven-fifteen, and a police chase at eight had the outbound traffic backed up a total of twenty-seven miles. The chopper jockey on WJR could barely contain his glee.

I was out of just about everything, so after Mary Ann Thaler left I sopped up the alcohol with toast and a fresh pot of coffee I hadn't strained through limburger cloth, boiled off the sweat and stink of Black Squirrel Lake with hot water, shaved, and put on a sport shirt, slacks, and loafers. It was Casual Friday in the detective business, but even that has its limits. I swung by the office to break the Chief's Special out of the safe and snapped it to my belt under the shirttail.

From there I drove to the old Kern block and entered a narrow deep shop in Merchants Row, a thirty-million-dollar face-lift on a ninety-five-year-old commercial neighborhood with loft apartments erected atop 28,000 square feet of ground-floor retail space, most of it filled with stepladders and draped canvas; when you build it they don't necessarily come. The clerk behind the glass counter was a kid who couldn't stop yawning. He tore off a bitter one and turned over the object I'd placed in his hand. "Man, you're not supposed to immerse these in water."

"Man, I couldn't help it. It was on me when I went through the wash cycle. Can you fix it?"

He opened the cell phone and shook out a jigger of water. "I can replace it. It'll cost you full price. You voided the warranty."

"I need to retrieve a number from this one's memory. Someone called me the other day and I have to get back to her."

"What day?"

"Wednesday."

"Come back Monday. No, Tuesday. Monday's the fourth."

"I need it today."

"Not an option. Frankenstein didn't build

Boris Karloff in a day." He yawned.

"I'm impressed. I didn't think anyone your age knew Boris Karloff from Boris Yeltsin."

"Who?"

I snapped a fifty-dollar bill under his nose. His mouth clapped shut in mid yawn.

I went out to smoke cigarettes and watch the tumbleweeds. The opposite side of the street was in deep shade but on my side the sun walloped the pavement. The parking meters shimmied and swooned and there was a sweet sticky smell of bubbling tar. A FedEx truck stopped in front of the old Parker block to make a delivery, then moved on, and that was the only human activity I witnessed until I snapped my last stub at the storm drain and went back inside.

The kid had my dead cell plugged into a laptop computer open on the counter. His hands fluttered over the keys. At least he'd stopped yawning. I admired the racks of fuses, coiled cords, and software on display while he diddled. Everything available seemed to have been made in China, with instructions in English and French.

"Okay, you want a printout?"

I put down a gadget that promised to transmit the sounds of Eminem to whatever radio stations weren't carrying them. "Just show me the screen."

He swiveled the laptop my way. I recognized Darius Fuller's number in Grosse Pointe and several others. I wrote the two I couldn't identify in my notebook. One of them would belong to whatever instrument Charlotte Sing had used to invite me to interview her at her temporary suite in the Hilton Garden Inn. "Thanks." I put away the notebook.

"How do you want to pay for that replacement phone?"

"I'll let you know."

"I can fix you up right now if you've got a card."

"I don't have a card."

"Personal check's okay. We know where to find you." He looked sly.

"I've got twelve dollars in checking. When I said I'll let you know I meant whether I decide I want a replacement."

"I can give you an upgrade if you're dissatisfied."

"I'll think about it."

"Man, you can't walk around without a phone!"

I hung a cigarette off my lower lip. "What do you think people did before cell phones were invented?"

"Same thing they did before cars: walk on

their knuckles and watch *I Love Lucy.*"

I went back to the office and tried the numbers. The first didn't answer and the second turned out to belong to the cell phone company, calling from headquarters to find out how much I liked my purchase. I'd forgotten that call immediately. The kid in the store could have told me what it was and saved me the trouble. I made up my mind then about replacing the cell.

I went through the mail. There was no change in my Hupmobile stock, so I tried the first number again. A female voice with a musical note in it read back the number by way of salutation.

"Good morning, Mai. This is Amos Walker. Do you remember me?"

"Yes. We played a little trick on you." Her tone didn't change. "I'm afraid Madame Sing is unavailable. She's leaving for San Francisco this afternoon."

"She offered me a job the other day. I'd like to give her my answer."

"I'll take the message."

"The answer is yes; which means I'm going with her when she leaves. What's her flight number?"

"I'm sure she didn't intend for you to start right away."

"If something happens because her security is shorthanded I'd never forgive myself. Anyway, I want to see how they celebrate the Fourth out on the Coast. A parade with a dragon float, I hope. I can make my own arrangements if she's booked all her seats."

"I'll call you back."

I told her my cell was out of order and gave her the office number. I hung up grinning. As Asians went, Mai was thoroughly scrutable. I'd thrown a curve and caught her looking.

The moment was gone almost before I could savor it. The hall door opened and I was getting up to open the private door when it swung around on its hinges and the knob punched a hole in the plaster on my side. Elron, the Scientologist bodyguard, stooped to look at me and stuck out what looked like a Takarov semiautomatic at arm's length. He'd traded his gray hoodie for a yellow Ridgerunner T-shirt that exposed most of his impressive superstructure. The heat had gotten to him finally. "Lay it on the desk."

I'd drawn the Chief's Special without thinking. I put it on the blotter and took a step back. "I thought you union types always looked for the label." I tilted my head toward the foreign pistol.

He looked at it as if noticing it for the first

time, then made a dry sound in his throat and lowered the hammer and the weapon. "Wilson don't supply the equipment. They sell this Russian military ordnance by the pound. Threw in a case of ammo free of charge. Okay." He stepped inside and away from the door.

They came in single file because there wasn't a doorway this side of Uncle Ed's Oil Shop that would let them in two at a time. None was as big as Elron, but all four of them in one place shattered the local safety code. Their faces wore the empty sightless concentration of the bodybuilder's trance: hour after hour pumping away in the exercise yard, nothing to listen to but the rattle of the weights and the whistle of their breath. They trundled in and stood with their backs to my walls, arms not quite hanging at their sides because the shortened tendons bent them at the elbows. Two were white; say what you like about Wilson Watson — and people did — he did his recruiting by the board foot and not on the basis of race.

"Okay, Wilson," Elron said.

Today it was urban upscale, P. Diddy instead of Fresh Prince. Watson had left the cap and leather jacket behind and turned out in a silver pinstripe and gray fedora with a black silk band, but he still looked like Humpty Dumpty. He waddled in on his broken-straw legs, looked from me to the revolver on the desk to Elron. "Check him for hideouts?"

"Nah. Man don't wear them in his own digs. They're uncomfortable enough outside."

Watson didn't like that, but he didn't pursue it. I learned something then: He was a little afraid of his own security. He'd picked it for size and punishing power, but he was still the sick kid hiding from bullies in the corner of the playground. It was a handy thing to remember.

"I'm short a man," he said. Addressing me for the first time.

"I just took a job. Try the Wayne County Jail."

"Somebody tipped Bairn that Ernesto was coming. He couldn't of got the drop on him otherwise. I heard you was there."

"I found Esmerelda. He looked just like a little angel."

"You found more than that, I heard. You let Bairn get away."

"I was distracted at the time. It hit the news, I guess. I missed it this morning. What do you know about Fred Loudermilk?"

"Who's that?"

"Okay, maybe they're sitting on him. He's lake security. He drew down on me and told Bairn to beat it. Later he made a more energetic attempt to keep me from going to the law. I dropped a pier on his head."

"Dead?"

"Concussed."

"Still?"

"Awake but not talking. How'd Esmerelda find out Bairn was hiding at Deirdre's mother's place on the lake?"

"I came here to ask questions, not answer any."

"If you wanted to beat anything out of me, you should've brought more guys."

"Nobody's that hard."

"Not hard. Pigheaded. My old man was a Teamster back when Jimmy ran the joint, and it rubbed off. By the time you get me softened up enough to talk, I won't be able to. There's another way."

"I didn't come here to negotiate neither. Christ, you got balls big as bazookas. I'll get 'em dried and hang 'em from my antenna."

"You can't pay me. I wouldn't know what to do with it any more than a dog that caught a car. I'm talking about truth or dare."

"Swap? Shit."

I didn't point out the obvious. Watson's

224

skin was thinner than his labor status, and he was too good an organizer not to know where his association was weak. Ernesto Esmerelda had known how much pressure to apply without getting carried away and destroying the source of information. Muscle without discrimination had no place on the table.

Elron stuck his Russian pistol behind his back. Leather squeaked. "I'll hang him out the window. Can't go wrong with a classic."

"We're only two floors up," I said. "I could chip a tooth."

"So I'll take you up on the roof."

"Shut your hole, Elron." Watson ran a thumb down the side of his silk necktie. "All right, asshole. We hold the onions for now. Bairn told me about the place on the lake when he was making his pitch about everything he had coming when he married the Fuller bitch. When that deal went south I sent Ernesto to look for him there. I thought maybe you figured the same thing and got word to him to expect a visit."

"What I saw of Bairn I didn't like strong enough to stick my neck out. Anyway, a guy with accounting training could work that out for himself. Maybe he saw your boy coming. It's the pros that get careless."

"Not Nesto. He outsmarted Castro's best

and he wasn't slowing down."

"There's another explanation," I said. "Bairn wasn't the shooter."

Watson stroked his soul patch, then shook his head. "Plenty of people didn't like him, but Bairn's the one with the connection to that house. And he was still hiding out next door afterwards. You saw him yourself."

"I didn't say it was a coincidence. If someone could tip him Esmerelda was coming, that same someone could furnish competition from Esmerelda's league. They parked Bairn next door where he wouldn't get in the way but where they could keep an eye on him, did the Cuban, and told Bairn to lie low until someone came for him. There isn't a mechanic in the business who'd risk being stopped with a fugitive in the car on the way from a hit. Ditching the body in Bairn's car and driving it into the lake sealed the deal, they thought; no wheels, no flight risk."

"They didn't know he had legs?"

"They thought they had him scared enough not to use them, but they overplayed their hand. He was scareder of them than he was of getting caught by the law and charged for Deirdre and Esmerelda. He was sure scareder of them than he was of you. That's why he took the chance of losing

Deirdre and his shot at two million and used her to hock a stolen watch to pay you something on account."

"He went to that chink chick for a loan and she told him to take a walk, that's why," Watson said.

"No. You got that from me, and I got it from her. That was before I found out how big her ambitions were. She wouldn't turn down any avenue of financing out of hand. She offered to bail him out. It was what she demanded in return that scared Bairn out of all his best hopes, turned him back into the small-time thief he was just to stay alive and out of big-time trouble. The kind of trouble that can jack you up for the rest of your life."

"Such as what?"

"She buys and sells people," I said. "Start with that."

TWENTY-ONE

Watson perched on the edge of the customer's chair with his feet spread in varnished cordovans, forearms on his knees, snap-brim shoved to the back of his head to give his brain some air. After a moment he straightened and snapped his fingers at one of the wrecking crew, who cut himself loose from the wall and dug out a thick fold of bills in a diamond horseshoe clip. Watson took it and sat fingering it. It seemed to be his rosary.

"What's Bairn got that the dragon lady wants so bad she'd off Nesto and buy this toy cop to keep him out of the can?"

"Loudermilk was bought already," I said. "I'd be guessing the rest."

"Guess away. Nobody here knows how to take notes."

I sat in the swivel. I wanted to stay on my feet in case Elron or one of the others broke his leash, but my legs were still rubbery from the lake. "Bairn's a bookkeeper for a courier firm. It could be she wanted him to cook the books and skim some off for her, but if he were any good at that he wouldn't be peddling stolen merchandise for quick cash. Anyway, if the scope of her operation's as big as advertised, she needs millions to grease the wheels, not the few thousand he might manage to chisel, and even if that was the plan it shouldn't have frightened him so much he'd jeopardize his meal ticket to pay his way out of the hole you put him in."

"Okay. So we know what it wasn't. What was it?"

"It's a courier service, don't forget. It delivers medical supplies and human organs all over the world by way of its own air fleet. It's a sweet front for funneling case dough to Sing's contacts overseas and transporting human cargo back home. No one has to know the planes don't return empty except the bookkeeper, whose figures would reflect the extra fuel consumption. If she tried to recruit him to cover up traffic in illegal aliens, just when they're top priority in Washington, it might scare him plenty. She didn't refuse his request for a loan; he refused her offer on account of the strings she tied to it."

"So you figure she offed his bitch to show

him she meant business. That's cold."

"That's something *you* might do. Maybe she arranged it to jam Bairn with the law so bad he'd have to agree to her terms to clear himself. She's got the pockets to lawyer him up tight, or she could go the simpler route and throw someone to the wolves to take the rap. Maybe the actual killer. Meanwhile, though, she'd have to keep Bairn out of official custody in case he talked. Owning most of Black Squirrel Lake as she does, Sing figured he'd hide out at Fuller's old vacation house. Your boy Esmerelda just happened to track him there when Sing's own enforcer was on the premises, explaining things to Bairn.

"It had to have been a chance encounter," I said, when Watson's head started shaking. "It explains the battlefield decision to stash Bairn next door until things cooled down enough to spirit him away. Otherwise he wouldn't have been within twenty miles of that spot when Esmerelda showed up. Sing would already have had him on ice."

Watson riffled the edges of the bills with a thumb, twiddling. "The shooter was in so much of a hurry he didn't give a shout-out to Loudermilk. So the toy cop let Bairn boogie instead of stashing him where Sing's peeps could finish explaining."

"More likely Loudermilk panicked when I showed. Holding two men under one gun for different reasons was just a little outside his area of experience. When push came to shove all he remembered was Bairn had to be kept away from the authorities. He told him to beat it while he had me pinned down, and now Sing's people are busy combing Oakland County for her patsy. It's a big county. My guess? She's put the same enforcer in charge who killed Esmerelda. If they can't throw a loop around Bairn long enough to make him cooperate, they'll cut their losses and plug him the minute he breaks cover. All it takes is one scared snitch to bring down a government or a corporation or an international conspiracy."

"He's the one I want. The enforcer." Watson slid off the horseshoe clip, skinned ten bills from the fold, and held them up between two fingers of his left hand. "Thousand a day till you find out who killed Nesto. Tell me, not the cops. And don't milk it. I got eyes all over town."

"Use them. Even if I worked for thieves, I wouldn't work for you."

Elron stirred. I felt it in my legs. I wondered if those big weightlifter's muscles would slow him down long enough for me to get to my gun before he jammed the

Takarov down my throat.

But Watson only looked amused. He rewrapped the bills around the fold and slid the clip into place. "Nesto and I go back. They stopped exporting his quality years and years ago, like good Havanas. You tell me your terms and we'll negotiate."

"It's timing, not price. When I deliver to my first client, the package will include the name of the shooter. Why not give your backfield a break and let the cops deal with him?"

"I thought Fuller would of shoved you off by now."

"He did. I'm the client now. I've been shot at and pushed around and almost drowned. It's *me* time."

The telephone rang. I let it twice, then picked up.

"Mr. Walker? This is Charlotte Sing. Mai gave me your message." Her voice was raised a little, the way people do when they're speaking on a cell.

"One moment, please." I cupped a hand over the mouthpiece. "We done?"

Watson rose, pushing on the seat until he had his weight distributed evenly on his toothpicks. "Anyone jacks you around, you tell him I got an interest in the concern."

"More Esmereldas?"

232

"That's the thing about unions. There's always the second shift."

The Village People preceded him out the door; all except Elron, who paused to scoop the revolver off the desk, shake the shells into his big palm, and toss them into a corner. Then he left, the Russian pistol riding a clip on the back of his belt. I didn't have a refrigerator there to tip over.

After the outer door closed I put down the receiver and got up to make sure no one had stayed behind, then went back to my seat and apologized to Mrs. Sing for the interruption.

"If you're indeed going to work for me, I have to insist you address me as Madame."

"It'll take getting used to," I said. "It has a different meaning in this country, as I'm sure you know."

"In my culture it's a simple sign of respect. Many of my employees are new to this hemisphere. If I preserve some of the old customs it makes the transition much easier."

"I'll brush up on my tea ceremony."

"I'm curious to know what made you decide to accept my offer. You struck me as a man who prefers self-employment."

"That's just another way of saying I've got a different boss every week. Also the travel opportunities are vastly overrated. Last month I was in Toledo three times."

"I think I can promise you something a bit less tedious. Not San Francisco, however; not today. I'll be back after the holiday. There is some briefing involved, and my schedule is tight."

"I was hoping to get away for a while. I'm still keyed up over the Bairn case."

"I heard about it on the news. Does this mean you're finished with it?"

"Just a couple of loose ends to tie off. I was hoping to do that on the plane if you weren't too busy."

"I? I told you everything I know."

"That's not what Fred Loudermilk said. Well, bon voyage. Hope they serve fresher pretzels on chartered flights." I cradled the receiver.

The telephone rang again as I was retrieving the cartridges from the floor where Elron had tossed them. I had a box in the desk, but I was thrifty and in no real hurry. One of them had rolled out of reach behind the radiator and I got up to get a pencil and tease it out. The telephone went on ringing all this time. It was still ringing when I finished reloading the Chief's Special and went to lunch.

■ ■ ■ ■

I ate at the Pegasus in Greektown. I didn't particularly feel like Greek, but I'd found a parking space nearby and just around the corner from police headquarters, which didn't offer a valet service like Trapper's Alley, although it does better business. I put away a plate of stuffed grape leaves, chased it with strong coffee as thick as Valvoline, refed the meter, and walked to 1300. I took my time to avoid breaking a sweat in the heat. I was in no real hurry.

John Alderdyce had set up camp at a desk out in the public ward, exposed on all four sides. The name on the trivet belonged to a sergeant on suspension pending an investigation into twenty-five kilos of cocaine missing from the evidence room. The inspector and Detective Burrough were bent over a multicolored pile of paper when I walked in. The third-grader wore seersucker, the other silk. If Burrough had put on silk, Alderdyce would have turned out in chinchilla, with diamond pendants on both ears. The pair seemed to be waging a war of sartorial one-upsmanship. It's what passes for morale down there these days.

"Don't tell me they broke you down

already," I said. "I just heard about the reorganization."

Alderdyce looked up from under his rocky outcrop of brow. "Ceiling in my office fell in and took out the computer and fax machine. I had asbestos in my iced tea. Who told you the department's reorganizing?"

I stalled, working my teeth with the cinnamon stick I'd scooped up at the cash register in the restaurant. "You can't keep a secret in a drafty old barn like this. Anything to it?"

"Not if the union decides to grow a set of testicles. What the hell were you doing staking out Fuller's neighbor on the lake? You said you were off the case."

"Curiosity. I saw a curtain move in the window and I followed it up."

"Without reporting it."

"Curtains move all the time. I didn't know it was a violation."

"If you'd told the sheriff's deputies, we'd have Hilary Bairn in lockup."

"On a slab, more likely. He's got an armed-and-dangerous tag out on him on account of Esmerelda."

"It'd close the case," Burrough put in.

"They don't close that easy," Alderdyce said. "I don't close them that easy." To me: "What'd Loudermilk have to say to you?"

"Bang, bang, bang. I think that was the order. I didn't like where the conversation was going, so I went for a swim. He talking yet?"

"He's still under observation for concussion and a possible skull fracture. They moved him to a security floor with sheriff's Lieutenant Phillips' men and mine at all the exits. Everything's awake but his mouth."

"That should tell you something," I said.

"His silence doesn't back up your version of what happened."

"Phillips said the same thing. You law types keep tripping over each other's lines."

Alderdyce scooped up a fistful of flimsies and shook them at me. "A bale of these arrived by messenger from Oakland County this morning. Another's on its way. We're going over every traffic stop and suspicious-person report filed with the sheriff's department since the sun went down day before yesterday, trying to match a description with Bairn's. Phillips' men found the boat he used beached on the north shore. Do you have any idea how many cars are pulled over and suspicious persons reported over a thirty-six-hour period in a county that size?"

"More than ten?"

He smacked down the sheaf. A loose sheet

drifted off the desk like a pink snowflake. "This is real police work, Walker. We get ten paper cuts to every GSW. We don't get to turn up our collars and stroll down the waterfront whistling 'St. James Infirmary.' I could pick up that phone and smack you with a Sullivan for that contraband Luger. With shooting involved, that's your license and eight months in Jackson for dessert."

"I didn't do any shooting with it. If I hadn't been wet and tired and scared I wouldn't even have bothered to wave it around. Loudermilk wasn't going anywhere under all that scrapwood."

"Felonious assault if he doesn't back up your story. Attempted murder if the prosecutor's got a hard-on that day."

"Property damage, too. Phillips suggested that. *If* Peninsular Realty presses charges, which it won't. It's going to come down on me from another direction, just like that pier."

That part of the room got quiet enough to hear termites munching the timbers. Burrough found his tongue first. "What the hell is Peninsular Realty?"

"Charlotte Sing," I said. "You've heard of her, probably, though chances are you think all she does is run hook shops and gambling hells. We just spoke over the phone. I pretty much invited her to come get me and give me the same thing she gave Ernesto Esmerelda."

TWENTY-TWO

"You kind of forgot to mention that," Alderdyce said. "Twice."

"I came straight here with it," I said. "Well, I stopped for lunch. I didn't have much breakfast."

"You never do. You like to hit the ground running and screw me over early. I'm talking about before. Charlotte Sing's name kind of never came up."

"I was sparing you extraneous detail. At the time it looked like she'd been dealt out of the hand."

"Except she hadn't."

"One of her companies owns most of the frontage on Black Squirrel Lake. I got that from Phillips and confirmed it with Violet Pershing, the local Peninsular rep. That makes Madame Sing the majority member of the property owners' association there, and security Captain Fred Loudermilk's employer. He'd answer to her for little things like aiding and abetting a fugitive from justice and the assault on the odd private eye."

Detective Burrough pushed back the brim of the hat he wasn't wearing today. "Odd is right. That's a stetch and a half."

"Tell me about the part where she didn't count," Alderdyce said.

I told him about Bairn's request for a loan and Charlotte Sing's response according to her. Then I told him the version where she agreed to the loan but tacked on provisions that frightened him off.

The inspector tidied the papers on the desk, smoothing the edges carefully with his palms, and folded his hands on top of the stack. They were powerful hands, well-tended but corded with muscle. A thumb against either carotid would black me out in less than a minute. "Tell me about the part where she's more than just the owner of gambling hells and hook shops."

I'd gotten that from Mary Ann Thaler. She hadn't told me to keep my mouth shut, about that or her interest in bailing Alderdyce out of early retirement; but then maybe she thought she hadn't needed to. "Speculation," I said. "She must be into something worse than that to put the fear of God into a punk like him."

"Keep speculating. What?"

"She travels a lot. She offered me a job with her security detail and said I had to be prepared to pick up and leave town on short notice. Since she charters all her flights, she doesn't have to mess with airport security as much as the rest of us, so she could be carrying anything aboard: drugs, weapons, stolen merchandise. Hopping state lines makes whatever it is federal. It scares me just thinking about it, and I'm not as close to it as he is."

"You used to be a better liar. And you know goddamn well there's no smoking in this shit hole."

I looked down at the cigarette in my fingers. I put it back in the pack. "Nervous hands. I said I was scared. I'm a staked goat and I don't even know what the lion looks like."

Burrough said, "What makes you such an important goat?"

"Nothing, if I'm as bad a liar as John says. I told her I talked to Loudermilk."

"Did you?" Alderdyce asked.

"No, but I paved the way for some honest blackmail. I said I was taking her up on the job offer. She doesn't strike me as the type that would pay it. No hits, no errors if she thinks I'm bluffing, but if she sent someone to X out Wilson Watson's boy Esmerelda, she's not the type to just shake it off."

"Maybe Loudermilk did Esmerelda," Burrough said. "If we can believe he used you for target practice."

"Could be. I don't think he's got the stones. He couldn't take me out when it counted, and Esmerelda made Castro's dignity squads look like *Police Academy Four.* She'd have a specialist for such situations."

Alderdyce said, "You've got a hole in your trap. If Loudermilk talked to you he could talk to anyone."

"I'd double that guard," I said. "Without him it's hearsay."

Burrough watched the inspector lift the receiver off the telephone on the desk. "You're not buying any of this."

Alderdyce dialed and asked for Lieutenant Phillips. He got someone else and gave him the message. He hung up and said, "Out on a call. What's all this got to do with what happened to Deirdre Fuller?"

I said, "Either Sing had her killed to put the screws on Bairn or she took advantage of the situation when it happened. I don't know what makes him so important; maybe his job." I told him what I'd told Wilson Watson. I didn't mention my most recent meeting with Watson. The story always seemed to work only when I left out Wilson Watson or Charlotte Sing. It was strung out so thin it wouldn't hold both their weight at the same time.

Alderdyce said, "Sing has her own organization in place if she's distributing contraband. She wouldn't need Bairn just because the company he works for deals in transportation. If she went so far as to provide a pro to shield him from Esmerelda, Bairn's important to her plans."

"What'd you turn on that pistol Fuller gave Deirdre?" I asked.

Burrough answered. "Beretta Nine. We turned up the paperwork in Lansing, but so far no piece. It's not the weapon."

I put a curious look on my face. The inspector dug to the bottom of a stack and pulled out a carbon.

"Ballistics took an unjacketed forty-four out of Esmerelda, probably fired from a magnum," he said. "More than enough to penetrate a door and still pack a wallop. Forty-four mag's the breakfast of champions. Twenty-two's strictly for closeup and forty-five and up presents an accuracy problem. They don't like semiautomatics because of all those ejected shells they spray around for the forensics team to find. Nothing in Bairn's background indicates he ever held a firearm, much less used one."

"Any theft on his sheet?"

"He hasn't got a sheet. All we've got is school transcripts and interviews with acquaintances and coworkers."

"Just because it wasn't reported doesn't mean he didn't jam himself up with the local pawnshops. They've got an Interpol all their own to identify fences." I looked at Burrough. "Did a man's watch show up in that bank box?"

"Nope. That was the lot."

"I'm worried about that watch," I said. "If Deirdre got mad enough to throw it at his head for mixing her up in a scam, it ought to have turned up at his place. Or in his car," I suggested.

Alderdyce said, "It wasn't in the inventory we got from Phillips. We talked to the pawnshop owners and clerks, by the way. They all had Bairn's picture on file. So all your theories aren't so full of shit as they sound."

"Thanks."

"I didn't say there wasn't a heavy shit factor. You've got Charlotte Sing all rigged out as Fu Manchu on nothing more substantial than a single conversation with the chief suspect in the Fuller killing."

"I've got more than that if she takes a swipe at me for what I said about Loudermilk. That's the whole point of why I'm here."

"Fine," Alderdyce said. "We'll law you up around the clock, or would you prefer something at County?"

"Both those things wreck the purpose of setting myself up as bait in the first place."

"Then what *is* the point of why you're here?"

"Professional courtesy," I said. "If one of those optimists drowning worms in the river lands a corpse that answers my description, you won't have to start the investigation from scratch."

He riffled the edge of the stack with the ball of a thumb. It sounded like Bairn's motorboat. "You don't hang yourself out like a piece of cheese for anyone but a client. Who is it, if not Darius Fuller?"

"That again."

"Again and again, till this whole historic pile of crap finishes falling down around my ears. And after that."

"Don't threaten me with County again. That's a summer rerun you don't want to sit through any more than I do. Anyway, you're curious to see whether I can get myself killed, and the chances for that are better on the outside."

Burrough said, "Jesus. Which one of you guys fucked the other guy's wife?"

"Walker's my best friend," Alderdyce said. "That should give you some idea of just how rotten my life is."

"Jesus."

"He had it a little worse," I said.

The telephone rang. Alderdyce speared it. I heard Lieutenant Phillips' voice but couldn't make out the words. Alderdyce said "yeah" a couple of times, listened for long stretches, then thanked him and broke the connection with a bang that made Burrough and me jump.

"That was Oakland," Alderdyce said. "Deputies found Hilary Bairn on the apron of M-fifty-nine, three miles from Black Squirrel Lake. Body's still warm."

Twenty-Three

I wasn't invited on a ridealong to the spot where someone had dumped Bairn out of a car where he was guaranteed to be found quickly, but then I wouldn't have seen anything the deputies hadn't and the Detroit police wouldn't, and in any case the story broke big enough to follow on the car radio and in the little portable TV I kept in the office. The cops weren't saying how he died, but there was enough blood on the ground — lovingly photographed by all three local crews — to indicate he'd taken a hit from a large-bore weapon. Since it was unlikely he'd been shot in such a public spot, it was too much for a small caliber or ordinary knife wound. I had my money on a .44 magnum.

Charlotte Sing, if it was she, wasn't letting the grass grow. However crucial Bairn had been to her operation, he'd become a ticking time bomb, more afraid of her than he was of the punishment that awaited him for killing Deirdre Fuller, and more likely than ever to talk if he were taken into custody. How quickly her people had caught up to him after he fled the scene of the Esmerelda killing and how long they'd held him before the order came down from the top to cut their losses and throw him to the maggots, we might never know. But I was sure my last conversation with Madame Sing had put the period to Hilary Bairn.

I didn't feel as badly about that as I suppose I should have, and not just because he'd panicked and killed a woman during an argument. From petty thief to gold digger to murderer was a predictable progression that ought to have been stopped a long time ago.

John Alderdyce's first act upon getting the news was to dispatch a squad of uniforms to beef up the watch on Fred Loudermilk at Beaumont Hospital. If Sing was slicing away all lines to whatever could drag her down, he was one of them.

So was I. But I was used to that.

I got out the office bottle, but just to hold; from here on out I was going to have to jump fast and run hard, and liquor's just for thinking. I smoked half a cigarette, put it out, and did one of the hardest things I'd done in my life. I went about living it.

Peninsular Realty had a quarter-page ad in the Yellow Pages, listing all its sales representatives in the metropolitan area with their telephone numbers. I dialed one.

"Peninsular Realty. 'If you seek a pleasant peninsula, look around.' "

I said, "You may hear from Lansing. I think the State of Michigan holds title to that jingle."

Violet Pershing recognized my voice. "Not really. What Lewis Cass actually said, and what the motto on the flag says, is 'If you would seek a beautiful peninsula, look around you.' Our PR people took advantage of a popular misquote. Did you change your mind about the treadmill?"

"I think they're illegal in Detroit. You're only supposed to use your feet on the brake and the clutch. Are you free for dinner?"

She put me on hold while she checked her calendar. "I'm showing a place up by Pine Knob at six-thirty," she said when she came back on. "I should be through by eight. Do you mind dining at a fashionable hour?"

"That's quite a hike. I didn't know your territory was that big."

"Ordinarily it's just the lake, but some-one's out sick. There's a terrific restaurant up there, if you don't mind the extra mileage."

"We'll meet there. Where is it?"

"It's hard to give directions to over the phone. Let's meet at the house and you can follow me from there."

"I'm a detective. I can usually stumble into a place if I walk a straight line."

"No straight lines lead to this place. Trust me, it's worth it. The ribs alone make up for the hassle."

I wrote down the address of the show house, said good-bye, placed some business calls, and wrote down the information, then threw away my notes. I figured I'd remember them. I went home to scrape off the day and put on my best suit, which was the only one I had left. It needed pressing; so did I. I'd had the coat cut long as usual and it hung over the gun without ostentation.

Going through the normal motions when you're the star attraction in a shooting gallery is as tough as walking across a stage without tripping over your tie bar. I didn't crack the curtains more than three times to check out the street and tried not to duck when I backed out of the garage and bumped over the curb, something I hadn't done in all the years I'd lived there. At the first stoplight I unholstered the revolver and counted the cartridges. There were five, same as three minutes ago. I swung the cylinder back into the frame and laid the gun on the passenger's seat where I could get to it without dislocating my shoulder.

I felt a little better when I left the surface roads and entered I-75 northbound. By then the air conditioner was running at full capacity, the steering wheel no longer felt slimy, and the area's constant state of rush hour had receded temporarily, giving me room to maneuver. You can keep a dogfight running a long time with several lanes to choose from and a thirty-mile-an-hour scale to slide up and down.

But the situation didn't last long. It was Friday night of a holiday weekend, and I'd dodged the nightly homebound traffic only to plunge into the glut of wild-eyed motorists bulling their way north to the straits and Mackinac Island and all the campsites in both peninsulas. Up past the zoo we slowed, then stopped, stuck at the bottom of the concrete drainage ditch south of Auburn Hills like grease in a trap. With the evening sunlight slanting in and the motors idling and drivers' faces turning red it was a hundred degrees easy, and I couldn't take the chance of keeping the air conditioner running and overheating the engine. I turned it off and cracked the window on my side, just enough to let in automobile exhaust and keep out bullets. One sniper up on the surface was all it took to turn the place from a junkyard into a cemetery. When a traffic copter puttered overhead I ducked again, then switched on the radio to hear what the guy had to say. No accidents, no construction, just plain physics. You can't squeeze a crate of oranges through the same strainer at the same time. I dialed up a classical station to flatten my nerves and listened to Chopin and the sound of my own sweat bursting out of my pores. Once again I counted the shells in the revolver. When I caught the passenger in the car to my left goggling, I grinned and showed the county star. The passenger, a woman in her sixties with a shag of pale yellow hair like a bathmat, settled back in her seat and said something to the driver, a man of the same vintage in a tam-o'-shanter with cocktail glasses printed all over it. He glanced my way, then tightened his knuckles a quarter turn on the wheel. Neither one of them looked like a hired killer.

One lane started inching ahead, then stopped, then another advanced a few yards. Cars crossed the line to join the express, passed me, only to be passed by me a few minutes later when my lane got the nod. Brake lights went on and off like marquee bulbs. It went like that for the better part of an hour. I made ten yards in thirty minutes. I hoped Violet Pershing didn't require punctuality in a date. The copter crossed back the other direction with jets running, headed for the hangar. Movement started again, the lanes took turns more often, we picked up speed. I passed the exit sign I'd been looking at since Tuesday. Then the flood broke and we swung around the long curve that slanted up and out of the bowels of the earth. A succession of truckers leaned on their air horns. I wound up the window and put the air conditioner on turbo. The sweat evaporated on the back of my neck. On the radio a pair of coloratura sopranos were scrambling over each other on the way up the scales; they sounded like casters mating. I laid the station to rest. Over on the oldies side young rockabilly Elvis was putting his hips through their paces in jail. I accelerated with him, on parole. I'd been stuck in traffic jams longer, but never as long as that.

I took the Sashabaw Road exit, coasting down to legal speed for the benefit of the occupants of a county cruiser parked on the apron. The holiday fundraiser had begun.

Pine Knob was built to match its name, a bump in the gently rolling landscape of a glacial plane, built with sand and fill dirt on a pile of junk cars with evergreens planted on top to keep it from washing away. Ski lift lines run up from the redwood-and-plateglass lodge at the base to the crest like thread to a bobbin, and in the winter when the snow machines are blasting rooster tails of blue-white crystal, the bunnies and hot dogs swizzle down the slopes, stomp their boots, and soldier back up to the bar on the second story, making as many trips as it takes before the place begins to look like Aspen. It's a beginner's hill with a liquor license, also an entertainment tax. There's a stage where spavined rockers and electronically enhanced country singers go to die. In the summer it's just a crumple of green pile and a gin mill attended almost exclusively by locals. I went past the half-dozen cars parked in front and followed the directions I'd been given through tree-tunneled roads paved with asphalt, clay, limestone, and corrugated earth, each of which was named after a lake. The country was rotten with them, and I'd had my fill of lakes. It was enough to make me want to move to Arizona and open a reptile house.

The sun was guttering, and the first dotted neon lines of fireworks showing against the purple, when I slid to a stop at the end of a glossy black driveway like vinyl and peeled my back off the front seat to stand in front of three thousand square feet of gold-enrod stucco and rosewood timbers masquerading as a cottage in an English glen, with hawthorne bushes planted in front and what looked like genuine mullioned windows on both stories. A Peninsular sign was pegged in the lawn. There was a red Taurus parked in the driveway. I'd seen it in front of Violet's house on Black Squirrel Lake.

I pretended to stretch while I stuck the Chief's Special in its holster behind my right hip and shook my coattail down over it. Then I stretched for real. Every muscle I owned was cinched tight.

The crickets were in voice, but I plowed a furrow of silence between them to the porch, small in proportion to the rest of the house but as big as my living room. It smelled of sawdust and fresh paint; the building hadn't existed at the beginning of the year. I paused with my finger on the button to read a peach-colored sticky note fixed to the door:

Amos,
   I'm upstairs, making beds. The cus-

tomer insisted on trying out all three. Make yourself comfortable in the living room.

V.

It looked dashed off in a hurry, slanting heavily left. I remembered Violet was left-handed. She would carry around notepaper and pens for contingencies, also a roll of duct tape in case a pipe sprang a leak.

Cozy English rooms are as popular in America as British cuisine. The entry was a great room with a coffered copper ceiling, opening onto a seating area that would accommodate twenty in front of a stone fireplace with flames in the hearth, at war with the air-conditioning. All the lamps were lit on a dimmer system to slow the traffic-harried heart, and someone, Violet probably, had been baking apples in the kitchen. Nothing in the manual had been overlooked to dress the place up for a customer visiting from a cluttered apartment reeking of grilled cheese and toast. Some coffee-table books, but no intimidating shelves of volumes, and no television in sight. A cedar armoire took care of that. The floors were ceramic where they weren't carpeted in deep plush and there were just enough antiques spotted around to anchor the place to the ground without appearing spinsterish. A lounging robe casually flung across the arm of a sleek blue leather sofa matched the rose lamp shades. The lady was an artist of her kind.

The armoire I'd thought concealed a TV turned out to be a completely furnished liquor cabinet. A pale pink fluorescent tube winked on when I opened the door, setting aglow rows of bottles on glass shelves, with most of the labels I knew and a few I'd never heard of. A flap swung down to function as a serving shelf, exposing crystal and stainless-steel barware. I slid out a cut-glass old-fashioned and poured an inch of Glen Keith into the bottom, just to straighten out the kinks.

"Oh, you found the bar," Violet said. "I forgot you're a detective. Can you make a Manhattan?"

I hadn't heard her coming across the thick carpet. Also she was barefoot. She'd paused to scoop the rose-colored robe off the end of the sofa and was tying the sash as she approached. She hadn't much on underneath; cologne, possibly. I'd missed the show.

I said, "I don't know. I never tried. Is that the outfit you wear when you show a house? You must make a pile in commissions."

"I got sweaty building that damn fire. If

I'd said in the note I was taking a shower, I might've scared you off."

"Naked women don't frighten me as much as they used to. Where do you keep the cherries?"

"Skip it, it's too much conversation and too little actual drinking. Bourbon and soda will do."

"How much fizz?"

"Sst. Like that. Fill the rest from the bottle."

"Aren't we driving?"

"I changed my mind about the restaurant. It was going to be my treat, but I didn't make the sale. I put some things in the refrigerator to make the place look homely. We can fix something later. Is that all right?"

"It's swell. I never did like following people when I wasn't being paid for it." I took another glass up to within a half inch of the rim with Maker's Mark, picked up a ruby-colored seltzer bottle, and leveled it off. When I turned from the bar she sat half reclining on the blue sofa, one bare leg crossed over the other. I take a special interest in attractive women's feet. How well they care for them says a lot about character. Hers were slim and ivory, the least bit long for her height, but the Great Wall had been standing a long time since Asians bound the feet of infant girls. I liked them fine. Not so much her legs; there was a little too much muscle there, like a ballet dancer's. I have a policy against going out with women who can kickbox me to death. I asked her if she was a gymnast.

"Does it show? I had Olympic aspirations when I was younger. I grew out of it; most people do, but in my case old training habits die hard. I still put in an hour a day on the infamous treadmill. Full-time athletes always seem adolescent, don't you think? No matter how white their hair or how bad their arthritis. Emotionally bonsai." She accepted her glass and touched it to mine when I sat down next to her.

"Darius Fuller spent money like a kid when he had it."

"My point. The other reason I lost interest was racial. When you're small and have Asian blood, people expect you either to work the pommel horse or be a whiz at math. I happen to have a head for figures. That was as far as I cared to go to reinforce the stereotype."

"I didn't think Asian when I first saw you. Egyptian, maybe. Old Kingdom."

"Just a couple of anachronisms. You look like you stepped off the cover of *American Detective*."

"I don't think there was such a magazine."

"Before my time. Pulp magazines *and* detectives. I don't see how you make ends meet."

"It's the same as real estate. People need what people need. How'd you come to work for Charlotte Sing?"

"Peninsular was the first place I tried after I got my Realtor's license. I thought a firm owned by a woman *and* an Asian offered the best opportunities."

"How'd you know she owned Peninsular? Lieutenant Phillips of the sheriff's department didn't know it."

"I did my research. We forgot to drink to something," she said. "A successful conclusion to your investigation?"

"If you're sure. I'm superstitious about toasts. Some of them come true."

"I don't know what that means." She drank. She looked like a kitten lapping at a saucer of milk.

I said, "I did some calling around today. I couldn't find a Violet Pershing registered with the National Association of Real Estate Boards."

"I wasn't Violet Pershing when I got my license."

"I thought of that. Violet isn't a common name among women who don't go on senior junkets to Casino Windsor. There were two registered. One was black, the other failed to renew her license after forty years in the business."

She reached up and set her glass on a table behind the sofa. "I didn't think I made that much of an impression this morning."

"It doesn't happen as often as it used to," I said. "Maybe I'm losing my looks. Once in a dozen cases, a beautiful woman I'd just met would purr and rub herself against my legs. It almost always wasn't sex she was after. That was just the common coin."

Her elongated eyes were shards of black ceramic, harder than steel. "Don't flatter yourself. We were pretty relaxed with each other that first time. I thought I could let my hair down an inch, forget I wasted my afternoon on a pair of looky-loos who never had any intention of buying any sort of house, let alone this one. You seemed like good entertainment. I lied about being a realtor. I'm just a real estate agent, a flogger without credentials. Are you going to report me to NAREB?"

"Nothing that drastic. Just the cops and the U.S. Marshals."

She shifted a little, drew the robe over her leg. She said nothing.

"You didn't come to Charlotte Sing looking for work," I said. "She came to you. She told me herself she hires her people first on their merits, then on whether they're Asian. If a licensed realtor with Eastern blood was all she wanted there are plenty of Asian names registered. You came with other skills."

"Man trap?" Her smile would frost a flower bed.

"Among others. I'm holding the bait. You don't stock a show house with liquor you can only get in Scotland." I sniffed the old heather in my glass, but didn't drink. I put it on my end of the table. "I don't think many moves ahead. By the time I find out I'm playing chess and not Parcheesi, it's usually too late. Meanwhile I have to fake it and keep my eyes open. I didn't put it all together until you showed up in that robe. Sometimes the camouflage calls attention to itself. But not in Esmerelda's case.

"It's no wonder he didn't see you coming," I went on. "He wasn't expecting a woman in a company blazer."

She'd been lounging with one arm dangling off the arm of the sofa. When it moved I reached for my holster. I had the revolver on her before she cleared the cushions with the shiny .44 she'd planted there.

TWENTY-FOUR

"I wondered how you'd worked it," I said. "I didn't think you'd put all your chips on one number, but you couldn't hide a pen knife under a kimono that thin."

She let the magnum slip back between the cushions and rested her hand on the arm of the sofa. "You might've been gay or impotent. Are you?"

"That won't work either. I've been called worse by my friends. Was the plan to do me right here or wrap me up to go?"

"Right here. I like things simple."

I shook my head. "You'd lie to the hangman. With a realty sign out front you never know when someone might come to browse. Better to pin me down until the reinforcements get here and take me out after dark. That'd give your boss time to land in San Francisco and be seen there."

"You're smarter than Bairn. He came straight to me after the deputies shifted their search away from the lake, just like I told him when I left him. He thought the enemy of his enemy was his friend."

"Murder wasn't his lay. Deirdre Fuller was just an accident. Or was that arranged? Not your work, I don't think. A lethal hit to the head without a weapon is a specialized skill, and you're too cool to have done it by accident."

"I wouldn't know about that," she said. "I wasn't in on that end. I only came in when it looked like he might run to cover at the lake. That was a lucky bounce. Madame Sing has us spotted all over to cut down on response time, but the job doesn't often come to the jobber. Esmerelda was my first real assignment since I came to work for her. I've made a lot more money off sales commissions than I did off that job. Actual rental fees."

"Deep cover's like that. No one can afford to maintain a full-time force of killers otherwise. But why take one off the leash on Bairn's behalf? What's a bookkeeper with a courier service have to do with smuggling illegal aliens into the country?"

"That's not my end either. The work's strictly need-to-know."

"Whose end is it?"

The ceramic shards she used to see

through took a sharp jig, then returned to center. Her will was as hard as her eyes, but she hadn't been able to kill the reflex. I leaned back to broaden my field of fire. I was too casual about it, too goddamned sure of my ability to adapt to a sudden change in the status quo. Movement flashed in the corner of my eye and my head went flying off my shoulders.

Twenty-Five

I welcomed the nausea. You have to accept it anyway if you're going to enjoy a mild concussion, and when you're throwing up you're not dead.

I'd experienced that lightbulb-in-the-throat sensation enough times to be able to swallow it and keep it down with my teeth gritted until it washed away with the tide. Light came dusky pink through my eyelids, but I kept them shut. I sensed eyes on me, and if I opened them, came either another knock on the head or The Speech, and I wasn't up to either with my brains trying to squeeze out through the throbbing pulpy patch on the back of my skull. Fortunately it's thickest there, a combination of scar tissue outside and calcium reinforcement inside, supplied by my own chemistry to fill the gap where the gray matter had shrunken away from the bone. It slowed my thinking, but helped protect me from some of the consequences.

I was reclined, not quite flat on my back, on a less cushy surface than the carpet where I'd fallen when I slid off the sofa. I remembered the falling and the dull impact at the end, then nothing as I'd plunged down knockout alley, a place I knew too well. I felt movement and the vibration of a powerful motor, and beneath that contact with a solid surface rolling away under big wheels. At least I wasn't in a boat. I'd hoped not to find myself on, under, or near the water for a long time.

Then came a kind of yaw, and a brief feeling of weightlessness as whoever was at the controls made a gentle turn, shifted gears, and fed fuel to the system. Air sucked at weatherseal and whistled around the corners. The surface smoothed out. We'd left asphalt behind and started up the concrete bed of the entrance ramp to an expressway.

Somewhere on the other end of what I pictured as a large flat craft, something thumped out of time with the beat in my head: a rap CD or a hip-hop radio station. That confused me for a moment, but as my brain cells stuttered on like a series of worn-out fluorescent tubes it started to make sense. It always does when the bad guys come with their own theme music.

Something, a crane or a robotic arm or a claw machine from an arcade, lifted my left wrist, pressed the vein on the underside, lowered it, and withdrew. I felt a thin sheet of fabric under my palm and beneath that steel decking. I knew what I was in then, apart from trouble.

"Possum deal's bogus, Walker. Your head's harder than the Takarov."

I recognized that voice, too high and reedy for the barrel it came from. I didn't open my eyes. "One more argument in favor of buying American."

The syllables didn't come out in that order. The beat of silence that answered told me Elron had failed to reassemble them into coherence. He raised his voice. "Coming around. Bop him again?"

"Certainly not. You of all people should know a blow to the head can be fatal."

"I told you I didn't have nothing to do with that."

The voice that had answered Wilson Watson's hyperthyroid general factotum sounded familiar, but I couldn't place it. It was mild, masculine, and touched slightly by the musical accents of the Far East. I'd heard it a long time ago, if not on the other side of the world. I opened my eyes then and found my face six inches from the

269

slender features and balding forehead of Victor Cho, the owner of the unlicensed casino standing on property belonging to Charlotte Sing in Detroit Beach. His blue tie and white shirt were the same heavy grade of silk. The eyes under the hooded lids were intense as the tips of a slender thumb and forefinger prised my own lids apart, right, then left. A pencil flash snapped on, throwing purple halos. It went out. He straightened, sitting back on his heels on the deck of the Hummer, and held up a hand. "How many?"

"How many you got?" This time it came out right.

"Seriously. There is a risk of coma."

"In that case, two."

"Two it is. Elron was right about your head. That doesn't change the fact I disapprove of deliberately causing cranial injury. I saw so many of those in Pyongyang. A criminal invasion of one of God's greatest miracles."

"Speaking of those, where's Wilson?"

"Present." Watson's voice drifted back a hundred yards, all the way from the rear seat. "A good labor leader gets out in the field."

"How would you know?"

"Shut him up, Doc. This here's my favorite

part. Bump it up." The volume went up on the radio. I felt the bass in my shoulder blades.

Cho nodded, then turned out of my field of vision. When he turned back he was holding a syringe.

I tried to sit up. Elron's icebreaker head pushed past Cho's and a manual typewriter struck me full in the chest. I fell back.

"Just a mild sedative, Mr. Walker." The Korean squirted a short thin arc of liquid from the end of the needle to bleed air from the barrel. "It won't hurt as much as the one you got from Elron." A hand a lot closer to human than Elron's touched my wrist with something soft and moist. A sting of alcohol pricked my nostrils. I tried to jerk my arm away, but Elron sighed and the claw machine closed on the wrist and jerked it straight.

"No need to be frightened," Cho said. "I was a doctor in my country." That last part sounded bitter.

It was a sharp needle. I didn't even feel it go in. The Hummer's fat tires left the earth and carried me toward Mercury.

I was back underwater, flailing my legs and doing wingovers and tucking myself into a tight ball to avoid the green phosphorescent tracers slicing past me from the muzzle of Fred Loudermilk's relentless Ruger. I was a better swimmer than I was when conscious, but something was clutching my ankle, slowing me down and spoiling my maneuvers. I tried to shake it off, but it was holding on as hard as one of Elron's big paws. I looked down into Ernesto Esmerelda's dead face, gray and slick as silver paste, bobbing up and down and side to side in the turbulence, the body refusing to let go. Sharp pain lanced up to my knee, and I knew then that with his last breath he'd nailed one of his hands to my ankle, using the hammer from his trademark black toolbox; I was bleeding where the spike had gone in, the blood making a long smear in the water, ideal for attracting sharks. I wondered, not entirely with zoological interest, if sharks lived in fresh water.

Just as the thought occured to me, something clipped my shoulder, sending me into a spin toward the bottom of the lake, away from the bullets but deeper into the black and in the opposite direction of light and air and life.

"Slide, Walker! Slide!"

This was Darius Fuller, the stud in the Tigers' bullpen. It sounded like good advice, but I didn't know where the bases were, couldn't see them through the murk, and all the time that dead man nailed to my ankle was slowing me down worse than the instant replay. I clawed fistfuls out of the black water, moving slower and slower as the bullets streaked faster and faster along their green glowing tracks.

I wasn't alone. There were faces in the water: Deirdre Fuller's, empty-eyed and frozen in anger, as I'd seen it the last time coming away from the pawnshop in Ypsilanti; Hilary Bairn's, Eurotrash fashionable even in death, with a boil in the forehead where Violet Pershing's slug had not quite managed to exit; and finally Charlotte Sing's, painted white like a geisha's with the jet-track eyebrows of the Dragon Lady's in a comic strip most of the world had forgotten, mouth open wide in laughter that pounded in my head in a hip-hop bass. Hallucinations only reinforce ethnic stereotypes. If it was a hallucination. Insanity yawns wide beyond a thin line where you can no longer separate fantasy from fact, as in reality programming.

When I opened my eyes this time, I was alone. It was dark, and for a long moment I thought I was still swimming toward the bottom of Black Squirrel Lake. My nostrils burned as if I'd been breathing nothing but water, but my throat was parched. I was cold. My arms and legs were as heavy as anchors. My left leg — the one Esmerelda had nailed himself to — wouldn't move at all, and when I gathered all my strength and pushed it in that direction, something dragged with the unmistakeable sound of metal on concrete, stopping with a clunk when it came to the end of its chain. I was shackled.

I was hyperventilating. I had no access to my lungs, only to a shallow pocket of air just behind my throat that would run out if I didn't break through to the stores beyond. I caught my breath and held it tight. My pulse hammered in my ears — a welcome sound, not only because it meant my heart was still beating, but because it lacked the hypnotic regularity of rap. I counted to twenty, my eyeballs straining out of their sockets, then let it out in a whoosh that smelled stale even to my own nostrils. I had a terminal case of morning mouth.

I sucked at the air anyway. It was proof that my lungs still worked, and consequently my heart. I'd given up on both for a while there.

Now all I had to do was explore the dimensions of the coffin in which I'd been buried alive.

I sat up. A boom swung down and smacked me in the face, but I ignored it; I'd had Sunday mornings that packed more punch. I explored my immobile leg, starting with my hand on my thigh and working down over the mountain of my knee to my ankle, stopping at the thing that restrained it. It felt slippery, not at all like metal, but heavy when I groped beyond it; a steel cable in a thick plastic sheath. I retraced it to my ankle and explored the dimensions of the bulk that rested there. A turnbuckle, nothing less ordinary than that.

I found the butterfly-shaped key that held it taut, gripped it in my fist, and turned. The world was locked no tighter in its orbit than that simple device. I wouldn't have had the strength to budge it even if I hadn't been seduced, bludgeoned with the butt of a Russian semiautomatic pistol, and had my veins pumped full of morphine, or some less organic substance that was about as mild as a buffalo stampede in a dynamite plant.

That was as far as my reserves went. I laid back to recharge, and as the thumming in my head receded I felt the more stylized throb of powerful engines, a thousand times more powerful than the one that had propelled Wilson Watson's Hummer, but without the comforting presence of solid earth rolling under wheels bound by the forces of gravity.

A boat.

Jesus.

No, not a boat.

A plane.

The whine of the jets was so incessant I hadn't heard them until I managed to eliminate every other form of transportation. If there's anything worse than drowning it's falling from a great height, aboard a craft that has no more business being in the air than a sperm whale: thousands of tons of sheet metal and wire and oil and fuel under high pressure and the iron smile of flight attendants that can plunge thirty thousand feet on nothing more substantial than a bubble of air in a rubber hose.

If, for any reason, the cabin should lose pressure . . .

What reason?

Should?

It was dark, darker than before the birth of the universe. There was no source of light, not one, and the air was colder than Michigan in April. Pitch blackness is not a modern concept. It breeds superstition of the kind that had forced Cro-Magnon man to look up from the mouth of his hollow in the rock and search for meaning in the black slab of cloud that erased the constellations and cry out for a Higher Power to guide him toward the light.

Where in the sprawl of modern civilization, under the million eyes of light pollution, even in the hold of an airplane, is it possible to find oneself in complete darkness? And why was it so cold?

Not the cold of depressurization at high altitude; I had a flash of panic before I came to that conclusion. People froze to death under those conditions long before the crash. It was unpleasantly cold, but not severe enough for frostbite. It had a man-made feel. There was a constant hum under the whine of the engines, regular enough to escape notice if you weren't alone in the dark with nothing to distract you from your sense of hearing: compressors. I was trussed up in a flying refrigerator.

I sat up, propping my back against icy fiberglass insulation, and patted my pockets. They'd taken away the Chief's Special, but they'd left me in my suit with my wallet and keys and change where I'd put them. I came to a cardboard fold, took it out, tore loose a match, and tried to strike it, but I was shivering and my hands shook and all I managed to do was demolish it. I let it drop and tore out another. This time I concentrated on steadying my hands. The flame flared white, receding to yellow as the sulphur burned off and the paper caught fire.

I held it up. The light only reached to the near wall, but I saw rows of odd-shaped boxes held in place on shelves by wire mesh. They had handles and looked like small picnic baskets.

The flame nipped at my fingers. I shook it out. If I was going to find something I could use to free myself, I would need more than a few seconds of light, but I didn't want to burn up the matchbook in case it came in handy later. You never know when you might take it in your head to commit arson at thirty thousand feet. I groped out my notebook, fanned it open, struck another match, and held it to a corner of a page. I figured I'd remember this case even if I burned up all my notes on it.

I passed my makeshift torch along the rows of boxes. They were nothing more exotic than portable ice coolers made of heavy-duty plastic. I figured I could use one to pound loose the screw on the turnbuckle that fastened the cable to my ankle, and as a weapon in case nothing better presented itself.

The mesh was open on top; it was only there to keep the cargo from shifting in flight. I transferred the burning notebook to my other hand and reached up to grasp the handle of the cooler nearest me. The light shifted and fell on a human face in the darkness.

It was less than two feet from where I was sitting. Startled, I dropped the torch, burning my hand when I snatched it back up to keep from going out on the floor. I changed hands again, sucked my fingers, and extended the flame toward the spot where I'd seen the face. A pair of eyes glistened through lowered lashes, but the light was only a reflection of the fire. Fred Loudermilk wasn't looking through them anymore.

TWENTY-SIX

The flame burned down while I was looking for a wound. I shook it out before it could burn my fingers. There would be a wound. He wouldn't do Madame Sing the favor of dying of natural causes, and if he had there wouldn't have been a reason to remove him from the hospital.

Why she had wasn't much of a mystery. Security can be gotten around or they wouldn't make so much of it, but pumping Loudermilk to find out who he might have told about her connection to the Esmerelda murder would take more time than kidnapping him; after that there would be all the time in the world, for everyone but him.

Putting the body in with me didn't guarantee me much more.

I went to work in the dark. It took me a minute to find the cooler by feel, but I got hold of the handle and lifted it clear of the mesh that held it on its shelf next to the

others. It was heavy, and whatever had been put inside to stabilize the temperature — ice, dry or the regular kind — shifted with a sliding sound, displacing the gravity as I was lowering it. Just then the lights came on, dazzling me; someone had opened a door or a hatch, letting in light from outside. I lost my grip. The cooler hit the floor end first, the lid tipped open, and something slithered out and across the floor, leaving a smoking trail of dry ice that seared my throat, choking me. The thing was red and quivering, the size of my hand, and when it came to rest against my thigh I felt the icy gelatinous surface through my pants. I recoiled reflexively.

A human liver.

I'd attended a couple of autopsies, and knew one when I saw it, although I hadn't much time to absorb the information, because Elron charged in, his weight actually tipping the airplane a couple of inches, knocked me flat with one huge palm against my chest, and scooped the organ bare-handed back into the cooler. Dry ice sizzled against bare flesh. He howled and grabbed at his hand. I braced my elbows against the floor and kicked out with my free leg. For a musclebound he had quick reflexes; he turned in time to protect his groin, but my heel caught him hard on the hip and he lost balance. He fell directly onto the smoking white pile that had spilled from the container, sending cooler and liver sliding and grinding particles of frozen carbon dioxide through his clothes. He whimpered and slapped at himself as if he were on fire, and as he twisted to get his feet under him the butt of the Takarov semiautomatic in the holster snapped to the back of his belt came inside my reach. I jerked it loose, found the safety catch with my thumb, and followed him up with the muzzle, yanking back on the action with my other hand and wasting a cartridge when it popped out of the ejector and hit the floor rattling.

"One in the barrel," I said. "Whoever taught you firearms safety?"

"This is a pressurized cabin. You want to kill yourself too?" He stood in mid crouch, breathing hard, his scorched hand tucked under his arm. Smoke drifted off his shirt and pants.

"Not if you stop the bullet. You're impossible to miss."

"And then what?" asked Charlotte Sing.

She stood eight feet beyond Elron, framed inside the arch of the open hatch. The light was coming in from the passenger cabin behind her and I couldn't see her features, but the small slender figure in the tailored business suit and low, lightly accented voice identified her like a thumbprint. I glanced at her only a tenth of a second and kept the pistol on the big man. I remembered his reflexes.

"Elron's right," she said. "There are five of us with the pilot, whom I pay. The only way to get us all is to shoot a hole in the fuselage. You don't strike me as the suicidal sort of hero."

"Maybe that crack on the head crossed some wires."

"I doubt you're that delicate."

I said, "You missed one."

She hesitated. She wasn't the type of person who liked to ask questions. "One what?"

"Watson, Cho, and Elron were with me in the Hummer. If they all made the plane, you and the pilot make five. You forgot to count Loudermilk."

"He's cargo."

"How'd you get him out of the hospital?"

"He had an incident. He had to be moved to another floor and there wasn't room in the elevator for a police escort. It's so easy to lose track of one patient in a facility that large."

That explained his dress, or lack of it. He lay naked in a soiled paper hospital gown.

"Who furnished the incident, Violet Pershing?"

"Mrs. Pershing was busy with you," Charlotte Sing said. "I have an acquaintance on the staff."

"Asian or occidental? No, that was unfair. Judging by Elron, your tolerance is spreading."

Elron said, "He was pretty far under when he got to me. I squeezed a little hard, but he squealed before he croaked. You're the only one knew Freddie-boy was working both sides of the street."

"He wasn't alone," I said. "Did anyone bother to tell Esmerelda you and Watson and Madame Sing were so cozy?"

"Nesto made an end run," Elron said. "Thought he'd lock down Bairn and deal himself in for more than just his day rate. But you can ask him how's that working out when you see him. You and Freddie are going for an ocean cruise."

"Which ocean?"

"Seriously, Mr. Walker, does it matter?"

I looked at the woman. "I'm hoping for the Pacific. I'm always on the wrong side when we fly over the Grand Canyon. Also I have a gun."

"Which as Elron and I pointed out is useless."

There was a control panel on the wall inside the hatch, mounted flush with an LED reading forty degrees. I figured it belonged to the refrigeration unit. I took aim at it.

Elron advanced a step. I shifted the pistol back toward him. "You first," I said. "Then I throw a log on the fire. I'm getting a chill."

"You won't shoot."

I moved the gun again and fired. The bullet passed through the end of a cooler on a shelf and traveled through two others lined up next to it before coming to a stop.

"Jesus!" Elron shrieked.

Madame Sing said, "That was an expensive point. You have no idea how much human organs bring on the international market."

"None," I said. "But I can always ask you for the latest quote. Let's hike it up a little. What's the expiration date when you turn on the heat?" I took aim again at the control panel.

"Stop!" she shouted.

It wasn't meant for me. Wilson Watson had come running to the hatch in response to the shot. He was back in ghetto mode, with a Chicago Bulls warm-up jacket, baggy carpenter's jeans, and a helmet liner on his head. He stopped his momentum with a hand on the arch. Victor Cho's face appeared over his left shoulder.

"Release him," Madame Sing told Elron. "We'll finish this in the cabin."

"Better make it quick," I said. "Didn't your old man ever tell you what happens when you leave the door open to the ice box?"

"He left when I was three, after setting my mother on fire." But he knelt at my feet.

The cable attached to my leg was fastened to a steel staple in the floor, part of a system built in to secure cargo. Elron took hold of the turnbuckle key in both hands. He had blisters on his right. He tightened his grip and took in his breath. His neck bulged, a vein in his acre of forehead stood out. The key turned a quarter inch. He exerted himself a few more times and it came loose. I pulled my foot out of the collar. I gestured with the Takarov and he rose and stepped back. A shudder racked my shoulders when I got up. It was warmer in the compartment with the hatch open, but my circulation was just getting started. My head hurt all over, not just where Elron had hit me with the Russian ordnance. Dr. Cho mixed a mean cocktail.

"Seat belt light's on," I said. "Everyone return to your seat."

Cho was the first to move. His hand gripped Watson's shoulder and the labor lug turned away from the hatch. Charlotte Sing touched a button on the control panel, lowering the temperature to thirty-six, and followed him into the cabin.

Elron started to back out, facing me. I made a twirling motion with the gun. He filled his chest, emptied it, and turned around to walk out forward, his shoulders up around his ears. He knew what was coming. I snapped on the safety catch, took the pistol all the way back, and swung it at an oblique angle to avoid hitting the low ceiling. The barrel caught him on the occipital bulge. He hit the floor hard enough to jiggle the plane.

TWENTY-SEVEN

"Was that necessary?" Charlotte Sing watched me change hands on the gun and shake circulation back into my hand. It had been like hitting a steel post with a lead pipe.

"Apart from the pleasure involved, it helped even the odds. I kind of liked him when I met him. Then he turned into a company man." I shut the hatch behind me, found the lock mechanism by touch, a spoked wheel six inches in diameter, and turned it tight.

"I lowered the temperature. He could die of hypothermia."

"Doubtful," I said. "It takes a couple of days to freeze a side of beef."

"I underestimated you. You looked too real to be authentic. But the odds are far from even."

"I'm not through chipping." I raised my voice. "Weapons on the floor, everyone. Kick them my way down the aisle."

Cho said, "I'm not armed."

Watson said, "Same here. I let Elron do my carrying."

"I've never owned a firearm," said the woman. "You can search me if you like."

"Maybe later, when we know each other better."

I decided not to search any of them. Patting people down requires time and close contact, and a gun is hard enough to hold on to without someone wrestling you for it. Anyway, if any of them were packing, another gun would have made an appearance when my shot had brought them running. It was a theory I had little faith in, but I was understaffed and out of my element.

Something crackled and a tinny voice came on over a PA system. "Everybody okay back there? I thought I heard a noise."

"What about the pilot?" Charlotte Sing asked.

I said, "A pilot with a gun is redundant. Give him the high sign."

She hesitated, looking uncertain for the first time in our acquaintance.

"Tell him what you like," I said. "What's he going to do, radio for help?"

"That would be awkward. This flight doesn't exist."

Heavy blue curtains separated the cabin

from the cockpit. She went that way, touching seats for balance, slid one aside, and leaned through the gap. A minute later she was back with me.

The plane was a twelve-seater turboprop. The passenger cabin was no larger than the cargo hold. That made it a courier vessel. That reminded me of something, but I didn't bring it up until we were all seated. Watson and Cho raised the arms on seats opposite each other and sat sideways on the cushions. I directed the woman into a window seat and perched on the arm of the one next to it so I could keep all three covered. We weren't as high up as I'd thought. Through the window showed the same checkerboard pattern of fields and forests you saw everywhere in the country. At least we weren't over water yet. I was becoming a full-blown hydrophobe.

"San Francisco's west," I said. "We're heading east, unless that bash in the head and the stuff in Cho's needle screwed up my internal compass."

"Sweden," said the woman. "With a stop to refuel in upstate New York and Scotland."

"Sweden, is that where the market is?"

She said nothing, profiled against the window with her chin on one knuckle. She looked like an ancient Chinese coin.

"Seeing that liver made me hungry for onions," I said. "It also answered the question that's been eating my lunch for days. Hilary Bairn worked in the accounting department of a medical courier service. That's what made him worth all the fuss. You wanted him to juggle the books to put your hands on transplantable human organs and laboratory paraphernalia. That's big money on the black market. It could finance an alien-smuggling operation on the grand scale for years. No wonder he ran scared."

She sat back and turned my way, crossing perfectly lathed legs sheathed in glistening black hose. She was a well-preserved specimen in her own right. I wondered how much time she spent in refrigeration.

"It's a squeamish subject for many," she said. "The scientific community deals in it like scrap. I don't bother with microscopes and serums; equipment is too bulky to transport for what it brings, and chemicals too volatile. You'd be surprised how many respected professionals, Nobel prospects, don't ask questions they don't want to know the answers to when it comes to raising money for research. That liver you spilled is worth two million in cash to someone who can afford to have himself placed at the top of the list of qualified recipients. Your own

Mickey Mantle got a boost, in spite of the fact his condition was self-created."

"He was your Mickey Mantle too," I said. "You're a citizen."

"You wouldn't know that by the way I used to be treated in stores. Of course, that was before I began making purchases in hundreds of thousands." She opened a hand as if to let something fly away. "Sweden is beautiful, but it's dark six months out of the year. Swedes consume more alcohol per capita than all of Europe, including Russia — which is our next stop after Stockholm. Cirrhosis kills more people in both countries than traffic accidents. Then there are corneas in Israel, kidneys in India, bone marrow in South Africa. In Sydney, Australia, a healthy heart would buy you twenty thousand acres of pasture in the Outback."

"I'm allergic to wool. If it's a bribe you're offering."

"Don't be ridiculous, you with your gun. You won't leave this plane alive."

Watson said, "She's fly, Walker. We're just passing the time on account of Elron forgot to bring magazines."

"Stop talking like Shaft or I'll put you on ice too. That was a nice fishing expedition at my place. You didn't want to find out who killed Esmerelda; you gave Madame Sing your okay on that because he tried to set himself up in independent business and you're a closed-shop kind of guy. When you found out how much I knew you tried to buy me off. That call I made to her was unnecessary. I already had the black spot out on me."

"She wasn't pulling your chain about the money. I put the screws to Bairn but good, for my cut. How'd I know he'd wind up offing his bee-yotch?"

I let him have that one. He was a cartoon.

"You're sure Elron didn't pay her a visit?" I asked. "Just to make sure the screws held? He likes hitting people on the head. Then comes the madame to offer Bairn a way out of the frame. Is Cho a lawyer, too? Maybe a sushi chef?"

Charlotte Sing said, "That was racist, and ungrateful. He chose merely to sedate you when others suggested a fatal overdose. Victor defected from North Korea, bringing with him a medical breakthrough from the hospital where he was head of research to endear him to your — pardon me, *our* State Department. He was given asylum, and later citizenship, but predictably the government back home was unwilling to release transcriptions of his qualification to practice medicine. He was delivering mail when I offered him a more respectable position."

"Spinning the wheel in Detroit Beach. I thought you only owned the property the casino stood on."

"No one can prove otherwise. About anything."

I scratched my chin with the gun sight. Three hours' growth of beard scratched back. That gave me a fair idea of the time I'd been in the Phantom Zone. I wondered if anyone was missing me. "On a second pass, Bairn got too notorious too fast because Deirdre Fuller was a secondhand celebrity. It made sense for Violet Pershing to save his butt when she saved it, but when the cops tied him to Esmerelda's murder and Loudermilk sprang him from me to keep him from talking, he became a two-time fugitive and hotter than a tin skillet. Back to Violet Pershing to mop up.

"So who stocked the refrigerator?" I jerked my thumb toward the locked hatch.

Madame Sing made a sound deep in her throat. "I had a backup. He looked less promising than Bairn, but he came through in the end. People generally do when there's so much money to be made."

"There's a lot of money in gambling too," I said. "There's a lot of a lot more in parting out the human body over two hemispheres; enough to buy up all of Australia, with New Zealand for a winter getaway. Not enough for you, though. The profits from the ready-to-assemble line are just startup to import the finished product into the U.S. What's next?"

She said, "People respect money. The more you have, the better the respect, and no one cares about the color of your skin or how many brothels you worked in when you were young and didn't know the language or the culture.

"I'm unique among the *Fortune* Five Hundred," she went on. "It's top-heavy with rags-to-riches stories, but mine is the only one that started with the rags on my back belonging to someone else, and me with them. When a slave becomes a queen, it's more than human interest in *The Wall Street Journal*. It's biblical."

After she stopped there was no sound in the cabin but the droning of the engines and the air whistling over and under the wings. We were over a large patch of water now: Lake Erie, if what she'd said about putting down to refuel in New York State wasn't some kind of blind. I switched the Russian pistol to my other hand, working my fingers as if I had a cramp, but really air-drying my palm. The weapon had grown clammy in my grip.

"Not about making money, then," I said. "Just keeping score. You're not the first foreigner who taught herself English reading clichés."

"Don't believe my press, Mr. Walker. I'm not made of ice. The numbers are shifting, didn't you notice? Hispanics are the largest minority in the country, well on their way to becoming the majority. Dearborn — Henry Ford's town, the birthplace of history's most infamous xenophobe after Adolf Hitler — shelters the largest population of Arabs outside the Middle East. They're streaming into western Europe as well; in London, the wailing from the mosques drowns out the bells from Winchester Abbey. Not so long ago, your own government — *your* government; I don't vote — became so alarmed at the hordes of Asians crossing its borders it established a quota system designed to reduce immigration of that one specified race to zero. I'm just balancing the scales. When I'm finished, we'll learn whether a yellow majority treats the dwindling white race any better than when it was the other way around."

I laughed. "Lady, you're nuts. I never figured to hear the Yellow Peril speech in my lifetime, let alone from an Asian."

"Amerasian," she corrected. "I've just enough of the devils' blood to borrow their methods."

Wilson Watson said, "Shit. I thought *I* had issues with the Man."

My stomach sank, but I wasn't afraid of Charlotte Sing, or even of the water now. The second smallest of the Great Lakes had slipped out from under us and we were over the patchwork quilt of New England, or New Amsterdam, or New Spain, or whatever the long chain of earlier immigrants had chosen to call it, beginning with the Indians, who'd crossed over from Siberia with no thought of conquest or wealth, just mammoths and mountain bison and new material for arrowheads. They were the only true minority left. The engines had changed pitch. We'd begun our descent.

I put the pistol back in my working hand. I was about to lose the biggest part of my advantage. In a little while, if it hadn't happened already, the temperature would rise dramatically, the pressure would become equal inside and out, and I'd have to shoot all three of them to maintain status, not just threaten to punch a hole in the plane. They realized it, too; I could feel it as surely as the change in altitude. And I wasn't alone.

Something heavy struck the cargo hatch

from the other side, hard enough to jar the plane from nose to tail; a shoulder, with 280 pounds of steel-tempered body behind it. The pull of gravity had revived Elron, in the hold with all those glands and eyeballs. The gasket held, but it squeaked. He'd back up for another try. I stood and backed across the aisle to widen my field of fire. I could feel the others bracing themselves for the rush.

TWENTY-EIGHT

But Charlotte Sing's first concern lay elsewhere. "You must let him out," she told me.

Elron hurled himself against the hatch a second time. Something cracked. She flinched. She was made of something softer than polished granite after all.

I said, "I guess it would take a lot of time to locate another plane with cold storage if he breaks this one. You might wind up with just a load of sweetmeats."

"What's the difference?" Cho asked. "You can't land safely with that going on."

"Okay, unlock it. Not you," I told Watson when he got up. "You two are a bad influence on each other. We'll let the doc do it."

Cho rose. His expression was tragic. "Please don't call me that. Without credentials it's just taunting."

"Sorry. Sensitivity's the first thing to go when you've been held down and drugged."

"I had no choice."

"You could have stayed a mailman."

"I'm a scientist!"

"You're a kidnapper and a smuggler. Open the damn door."

"Victor," Charlotte Sing said.

That trumped him. He crept down the aisle, took hold of the wheel, turned it, and backed away hastily to avoid being struck when it swung open from inside.

Elron paused with one hand on the hatch while he waited for his pupils to catch up with the light in the cabin. Then he saw me and charged. I fired at his feet. A hole opened in the floor. New York State whistled.

It stopped him, but it was obvious to everyone now that depressurization was no longer an issue. I spoke fast. "Sit down and strap yourself in, all of you. Ladies first when the shooting starts. No boss, no payroll."

Elron hovered, clearly in the no-man's-land between complying and drawing my fire. I didn't know how many the foreign piece held, or how many it would take to stop him.

"Go for it, Elron," Watson said.

The big man was fast from a standstill, blocking out the woman as a target as he pounced. My finger flexed on the trigger.

Then the floor tilted forty-five degrees and I snapped one off that missed Elron and shattered a window. The glass striated, then caved in to the wind pressure from outside. The engines yawned with the sudden change in course. I grabbed for the back of a seat, missed that too, and fell sprawling across that seat and the one next to it. I didn't know if the maneuver was pre-arranged between Madame Sing and the pilot or if he was reacting to the sound of the earlier shot, but he dipped the other wing just as sharply and I tumbled to the floor, hitting my elbow and numbing my arm and hand. The gun sprang free, struck the carpet, and skidded between the seats opposite, thumping against the side of the plane.

There was a general scramble then. Cho and Watson went for the weapon, Charlotte Sing bounded up to secure the hatch before her cargo could jump its traces and spill out of climate control, Elron launched himself at me straight from his heels, his huge glandular mistake of a body eclipsing the light as he fell on me with all his weight and encircled me in his arms. I twisted, catching him under the chin with the point of a shoulder and clapping his mouth shut with a crunch of enamel and a sudden spout of blood from one corner; he'd bitten through his tongue.

But pain is part of a lifter's everyday life. He grunted but ignored it, and with his chin glistening red he flexed his muscles and brought his hands together under my back. Once he'd laced his fingers there would be no letting go, even in death. He had the primitive physical mechanics of a snapping turtle. With all the life bled from him he'd still manage to squeeze me as empty as he had Fred Loudermilk.

Gasping for air I got a hand on either side of his tree-trunk neck and pulled, trying to slam his head against the steel leg of the seat bolted to the floor next to me. It didn't budge. The swollen muscles were as hard as tractor tires. I shifted my target to his eyes and gouged at them with my thumbs. I knew it wouldn't stop him, even if I routed them clear out of their sockets. It was just something to kill time while I waited for him to crush me to death.

His hands met under me, interlocked.

He flexed again. Plates shifted in my chest. Surf pounded in my ears. My vision tattered at the edges and turned black.

He let go. He breathed a chestful of hot air into my face and went as limp as a bag of rocks.

I heard the report then, or rather the echo, ringing like an iron bell in the aluminum can of the fuselage. I opened my eyes. The blackness faded, the blurring cleared. I saw Victor Cho's tragic face near the ceiling. I couldn't see the Takarov, but I knew who'd won the race to get his hands on it.

"No more murders," he said. "I lost my license, not my oath."

The plane pitched again, less dramatically this time, and an elbow in a Bulls warm-up jacket struck the Korean on the side of the head. He slid out of my line of sight.

"Chink bastard." Watson's voice. "I raised Elron from a pup."

Charlotte Sing said, "Never mind that. Finish it."

Then I lost sight of Watson too and knew he was stooping to retrieve the gun Cho had dropped. I shoved hard, but Elron lay on me like fresh cement. I wanted to crawl the rest of the way under him for shelter.

Instead something a lot harder than Elron plowed into me from behind and beneath, flattening my lungs between it and him. Other blows followed, rattling my organs and chattering my teeth, and from instinct I let go of the big man and shoved my palms against the floor to hold on. The world tilted, then reversed itself, tilting more steeply the other way, seemed to hang there like a drop on the end of a stalactite, trying to decide whether to fall or stay put and calcify. Finally it made up its mind and heeled on over, groaning and grinding and crunching, steel and glass and plastic all alike. Elron broke gravity and floated up and away from me, toward the ceiling. Then the floor came away from my hands and I reached up to grasp him again and ride him like a raft. We weren't defying the pull of the earth, just obeying it. He spat a stream of blood from his torn tongue when he struck, stinging my eyes, but he broke my fall. The plane had turned a somersault and finished on its back.

I'd blacked out again, I didn't know for how long.

That was getting old, and so was I. When everything else slows down, your brain is all you have left, and mine had been abused by the butt of a pistol and Dr. Cho's Magic Elixir. I'd voided the warranty.

I did a systems check, starting with my toes. Everything seemed to be working until I realized I was lying on top of a dead man, tried to roll off him, and stuck myself with a cracked rib. The sharp pain made me gasp, but the fog cleared and I levered myself to my feet, holding onto my side with one hand and grasping the edge of what used to be an overhead luggage compartment with the other. I was standing on the ceiling. I felt like a fly.

Elron lay on his back, arms and legs spread like a Dutch windmill, eyes and mouth wide with blood caked between his teeth. It was an obscene a thing as I'd ever laid eyes on. He'd disappointed me at the finish: almost three hundred pounds and six and a half feet from the floor to the crown of his head, and all it had taken to stop him was a bit of metal no bigger than a cashew, fired by a man half his size who'd sworn an oath not to cause harm. Aside from the part about trying to crush me to death, I still sort of liked him.

I went exploring, still holding my side and stepping over the dumped-open doors of the luggage compartment and the bags that had spilled out, including a matched set of Louis Vuitton that probably belonged to Charlotte Sing. I made a long leg to clear a bulky duffel and realized when I was straddling it that it was Victor Cho, with his head tucked under one arm like a sleeping seagull's. I didn't bother to stoop and check for a pulse. There wouldn't be one in a neck that obviously broken. He must have landed on his head when the plane tipped over.

There was no sign of the pistol he'd used to shoot Elron. I remembered then that he'd lost possession of it to Wilson Watson. I kept my eyes open after that, cast them up and down and from one end of the passenger cabin to the other. The hatch to the refrigerated storage room was still shut. I bent down, stabbing myself in the side again, and went through bags looking for a weapon. I found a portable hair dryer in one of the Louis Vuittons, wound the cord around one wrist, and let the weight of it dangle from my right hand. I figured I could swing it like a mace if I had to. I felt a little less pathetic, but not much.

Making my way through the fuselage, the passenger seats above my head, I found myself growing dizzy from vertigo. I couldn't tell for sure if it was me or the world that was upside down. Chalk up shock under the lingering effects of concussion and drugs. I leaned against the wall until the sensation passed, then pressed on. I wasn't going to turn my back on that plane until I was sure I was the only thing moving around in it.

I gripped the cord tight as I stepped over the crumple of blue curtains into the cockpit. My face nearly collided with someone else's and I jumped back, lacerating my side with fresh pain and bumping my already aching head against the edge of the opening.

The face was upside down, the eyes rolled back so that they seemed to be staring at the ceiling. The owner was a blonde, crew-cut Marine type, about thirty, in a white uniform with striped epaulets. He was still strapped in the pilot's seat, twisted half around from the shattered windshield to face the back of the cockpit. The hub of the steering mechanism had crushed his chest when the nose of the plane struck earth, pivoted, and slammed the craft down on its back.

I was alone with a cargo of dead men.

The hair dryer seemed more foolish than ever. I unwound the cord and let it drop. Neither Wilson Watson nor Madame Sing would bother to wait around once they got free of the wreckage. Police would be on their way with the fire department and ambulances soon or sooner, depending on where we'd crash-landed, and all the crooked millions in the world couldn't stop the ripples from spreading once the corpses were discovered and the cargo hold opened.

I wasn't through shopping, however.

Breathing shallowly to keep my broken rib from pinching my lung, I reached up and worked a rectangular metal case free of the control panel that had caved in on impact and pinned it against the console between the pilot's seat and the one reserved for a copilot, found the latches, and tipped up the lid. It was a map case, containing navigation charts and a month-old copy of *Playboy.*

I cast it aside, groped among the smashed dials and useless switches, opened a compartment, and took out a short length of pipe attached to a handle with a trigger in a guard, painted fire-bucket red.

The flare pistol went with me when I left the cockpit. I was still on the case, even if it no longer held any resemblance to the one I'd signed on for. I didn't know what kind of head start Sing and Watson had, but a signal fired in the air would bring out reinforcements a lot faster than if I went looking for them.

The emergency exit door was missing. It operated on an explosive cartridge that blasted it free when it was unlocked from inside. That was the path they'd taken. I tucked the flare gun under my belt, stuck a leg out into open air, and twisted to grasp the edge of the opening and lower myself to the ground, grinding my teeth against the pain that shot cartoonish red lightning bolts from my side. They struck again harder when I dropped to my feet. I nearly turned an ankle on a hard fibrous clump sticking up out of plowed caked earth: the stub of an old cornstalk. We'd landed in a disused field, where the wheels had caught on stalks or in a furrow and pitched the plane forward at high speed and into a cartwheel.

I tripped on the stalk, but I caught myself with a palm against the fuselage. It burned my hand on contact. It was the weekend of the hottest Fourth of July in years and the white-painted metal had been baking in the sun for some time. I fanned my palm to cool it and looked for bearings. The sky was scraped clean of clouds and there was nothing between it and the earth but a line of trees three hundred yards away on the edge of the field. If the farm still existed, the house and outbuildings would be on the other side of the plane. I hobbled alongside it toward the front.

"Too hot for a hike, Walker," Wilson Watson said. "Come sit with me in the shade."

I turned, grasping the handle of the flare pistol. I'd missed him in the pool of shadow under the wing. His back was propped against the fuselage and his legs, his pathetic stunted legs, were spread out on the ground in front of him. The left leg of his baggy jeans was torn, stained dark, and a shard of polished bone stuck out of it. Blood smeared the lower half of his face, congealed in his Fu Manchu moustache. His nose was smashed and both eyes blackened. He had to support the Russian semiautomatic in his right hand with his left wrapped around his wrist.

It was pointed at me. But then guns generally are.

He gestured with it toward the flare pistol. "You don't need that. Don't rush the Fourth."

I took it out of my belt and tossed it aside.

TWENTY-NINE

I regretted the loss, but not for long. In the next second I smelled fumes. The plane's tank had sprung a leak and dumped out what smelled like fifty gallons of high octane. It would take a lot less than a flare to set it off.

"That must have stung." I pointed to his shattered leg.

"I didn't know it was that long of a drop." He snuffled up snot. "Busted my nose too, when we hit. You took a bang too, looks like."

I was holding my side. "Just a rib. I've had so many of those I don't even let them tape them up anymore. They take just as long to heal either way."

"You don't count ribs. Know who said that?"

"The Cajun Chef?"

"Dick Francis. He was a steeplechase jockey in England. They take a lot of spills, through his smashed nose. I thought about telling him. Instead I sat down. Clumps of hard earth shifted underneath my tailbone.

"Hell," he said, "I know she ain't coming back. I knowed it when she said she was, but I don't know how many shells this commie piece holds. I got to save at least one."

"I wouldn't have typed you for a suicide round."

"Well, you be right. I figure to take one with me when they come. The rest'll take care of the rest." He grinned then, and it wasn't much better than when he scowled. His nose had started up again and the blood was dripping off his chin. "Hell, might be you I take. We won't neither of us know till the sirens start."

"You could throw down the piece when they tell you. They've got some pretty good therapists in the Jackson infirmary. You'll be playing basketball in the exercise yard by Christmas Eve."

"You ever been in?"

"Short time."

"Then stop talking about shit you don't know the first fucking thing about. It ain't what they tell you it is. It's a hell of a hell of a lot worse."

I thought I heard sirens. The wind had come up; it might have been whooshing through the trees.

"You should've stuck with that ATM scam, Wilson. You change your lay, you change your luck."

"I been running on bad luck my whole life. Be surprised what kind of mileage you get."

"Why don't you give me the gun?" I said. "You can unload it first. No one has to know you killed Cho. It's Elron's gun."

"That was uncool. I liked Elron but it wouldn't bring him back. What about Loudermilk?"

"That's a little different. He was bent, but he used to be a cop. Cops have this brotherhood, like the Masons. But that was Elron too. He might've gone off on a bender like Esmerelda. You could turn state's evidence on the smuggling charge and duck prison entirely."

"Sure, and you'd back me up."

"All I care about is who killed Deirdre Fuller. I know it wasn't you or Elron."

He wasn't listening again. "You hear sirens?"

"They're a long way off. I think we're pretty far out in the country."

"Where you think, Canada?"

"Not if my high school geography took. Buffalo, maybe. That area."

"Buffalo ain't country. I left school at fourteen but I remember that much." He stroked his leg. Then he seemed to remember something and dove into a jacket pocket. He came up with a Blue Diamond box, slid it open, and plucked out a joint, as brown and wrinkled as a justice of the Supreme Court. "I'd offer you a toke, but a busted rib don't rate."

I thought about the fumes again. I lifted a hand and let it drop. "I don't use it. You wouldn't have a flask in there someplace."

"Don't use it." He groped in the box and tossed it away. "Wish I'd left a match in it." He slid the joint along his bottom lip, tasting it. "No shit, you stuck on account of Fuller's daughter?"

"There was a little more to it."

He hawked long and loud, turned his head, and spat out a glutinous red mass that held its shape when it struck the ground. "Man, that's nasty. I don't guess letting a horse step on your face is a hell of a lot worse than smacking it into the side of a plane."

"A thing like that could put you off flying."

"Them sirens sure sound close." He tightened his grip on the pistol.

"We've got ten minutes."

"How come you know so much?"

"I grew up in a country town. Sounds carry out in the open."

"I hate the country. I never seen a cow till they took me out I-Ninety-Four in the van. Ugly motherfuckers. I ain't drunk a drop of milk since."

"You could ask for Milwaukee, it's a lot like Detroit. The feds really want Charlotte Sing. They'll set you up there with a new name and a job in a brewery. You'll have the place organized in no time."

"They got casinos there? My kind, I mean. The legit operations are too tame. Old people in sweats."

"I wouldn't be surprised. Everywhere people breathe they gamble."

He sucked on the joint, caught his throat just as if it were lit, made an unsatisfied face. "Christ, I'd kill for a light."

I made a decision. "I've got one."

"Shit, why'n't you say that before? Give."

I started to get up. The pistol jerked. I subsided, reached into my pocket, and brought out the book of matches. I hesitated, then flipped it toward him. It fell short of the knee of his broken leg. He grunted, reaching for it, then fell back, sweating. I stood, scooped it up, and held it out. He snatched it from my hand, gestured with the gun. I went back to where I was sitting and sank onto my haunches.

He opened the flap and laid the pistol in his lap to grope at a match. I did the calculus and came up short. He was a lot closer to the weapon than I was.

He tore a match loose, looked at me out of his bruised sockets. "How much is there to it?"

"What?" My eyes were watering. I couldn't believe he couldn't smell anything. I was afraid to move in case my belt buckle scraped the tab of my fly and made a spark.

"When I axed you why you stuck on account of Deirdre Fuller, you said there was a little more to it. How much more?"

"Not much. I've got a friend who's a Detroit cop. He needed the collar."

"Far fucking out. Cop in the pocket's worth two in the bush." He placed the match against the scratcher.

"I'm not going to tell him it was me set it up."

He looked up, poised to strike. "Why the hell not?"

"It's complicated."

He relaxed, lifting the match from the scratcher. The joint dangled from the corner of his lip. I sat back an inch, loosening cramped muscles. "Complicated? Shit, what's complicated about it? You got a cop by the balls, you squeeze 'em for whatever comes out."

"My game's a little different from yours. Like pro ball and college."

The sirens changed pitch, whooping as the emergency vehicles left the road and started across the roller-coaster surface of the ancient furrows in the field. He laid the book and the match in his lap and picked up the pistol. "Same game, man. What's the play?"

I leaned forward on the balls of my feet. "It's like you and Elron. Uncool."

The ruined face set into a bloody mask. His finger whitened on the trigger. Then it relaxed. He made a chuckling sound in his throat, hawked one clear from the back, and spat a long stream laced with red and yellow. He swiped the back of his hand across his mouth, smearing it with blood, and picked up the matchbook. He tore off a fresh match. "Shit. You're going to die piss-poor and dumb as dogshit." He struck a flare of white flame.

I was halfway up at the scratch and spun and launched myself away from the plane as the match caught fire. Then everything was taken out of my hands. A volume of

Mary Ann Thaler looked jazzed. That was always a treat. "Canadian Customs caught Violet Pershing on the Ambassador Bridge," she said. "They're extraditing. I get to help relocate her when she spills everything she knows about Peninsular Realty. You're looking extra crispy today," she added.

"You should see the other guy." I lowered myself into the chair in front of her desk. The burned spots were healing nicely, but the rib was still giving me trouble.

"I have, all of them. The coroner's people had them lined up in a barn in Lackawanna County; what they managed to separate from the nonorganic material that burned with them, anyway. They've identified the pilot, who'd just had his license restored after DEA nol-prossed on drug charges — lack of evidence — and Victor Cho, whose prints were on file with the State Department, on the basis of a surviving finger. So far there's just your testimony about the identity of the others. The one you said was Wilson Watson was close to the center of the blast, and so far there's no lead on Elron No Last Name."

"They met in Jackson. You'll find him in the records."

"Not the general you. Me. As the junior member of the team I get to sort through the dust bunnies in the file room. Watson and his homies served their time before computers."

"Wear old clothes. You get used to them." I took out a cigarette and fished a throwaway lighter from my sport coat, a rusty orange item I'd been shoving around in my closet since it went out of style. The lapels were as wide as French doors.

"No smoking here."

I put everything away. *Here* was an unventilated chamber on the eighteenth floor of the MacNamara Federal Building in downtown Detroit, with bare drywall and a track light hanging above a desk made of regurgitated material, and it wasn't even hers. She had it on loan for the conversation from the next head up on the totem pole, who'd inherited it from a Xerox machine.

"If you'd come to me, I'd have put a tracking device on you and we'd have Charlotte Sing downstairs," she said. "Instead she flew from Buffalo to Quebec on a driver's license and birth certificate in the name of Jennifer Yin and vanished in the Canadian northwoods. Judging by how conscientious our neighbors to the north are about keeping terrorists from crossing into the U.S., I'd say she's sleeping off the jet lag in a country without an extradition treaty right now."

"They play good hockey," I said. "Watson or Elron would have found the tracking device while I was out and buried us both up in Oakland County. Then Madame Sing would be on her way around the world, distributing black market body parts like sugarplums and trading them for fully assembled illegal aliens. I went to John Alderdyce and told him I was a target," I added. "That was the deal. You wanted him to get the collar and the credit."

"On the Fuller murder. Not Sing. Sing was ours."

"I said I might have to bring her in too."

"I thought you were kidding."

I said, "This is a communication problem, and it's not mine. John put men on me, they lost me in the crush on I-Seventy-Five. It was someone's responsibility at Thirteen Hundred to notify the feds that Detroit was conducting an investigation that included Charlotte Sing. Someone did, in last night's *News.* This morning in the *Free Press* he didn't. Which is it?"

"We're looking at that. Ever since the Big Shuffle, all the Washington and local agencies have been instructed to cooperate, but you don't reverse a decades-long game of Hide the Sausage overnight. So far it looks like John went through the chain of command. Whether the broken link occurred down on Beaubien or inside the Beltway is what we're trying to find out. Congress will probably get involved after the internal investigation finishes, and somebody with his pension securely in place will be retired publicly, and Sing will still be out there, rebuilding her organization stone by stone. Then we'll have to start all over again."

"Job security. Speaking of which, how does John's stand?"

"So far it's standing, no thanks to you. The DPOA has pledged to go to court to block the department reorganization and protect the rank and file from demotions and layoffs. There's no love lost between the mayor and the Hall of Justice, so the judge will probably issue a restraining order. He's safe until the city goes in debt another million dollars, which should be about next week."

Independence Day had come and gone while I was in the Lackawanna County General Hospital, recovering from burns and concussion, and multiple sprains; you don't count ribs. I didn't mind having missed the fireworks. The heat wave had turned into a tide, with no rain on the radar to push it back out, and with the door closed for privacy and no access to the air-conditioning ducts the closet felt like a Dutch oven. Not that you could tell it by looking at U.S. Marshal-in-Training Thaler: Her gray silk jacket and dark blue shirt-and-tie set were crisp and there wasn't a bead of perspiration in her backswept hair. She wore reading glasses for the benefit of the field reports she had spread out on the desk. That made her the Mary Ann I remembered, a sexy librarian who looked as if she might be persuaded to take out the bobby pins under the right circumstances. So far I hadn't found them.

She held up a report. "Last week the CEO of an organ bank in Southfield filed a ten-million-dollar claim with the insurance company because of a faulty thermostat. We've got a court order demanding he produce the spoiled inventory. We'll settle for five years in Milan and evidence of his deal with Charlotte Sing. Ten million, that's how much your little wienie roast cost the world in transplantable organs."

"According to her it was worth more on the black market."

"Think you're a good trade for the potential loss in life?"

"Somewhere there's a drunken Swedish industrialist who might ask the same question."

"Inspector Alderdyce asked me to call him when I'm through with you. You have some things to talk about." She took off the glasses, folded and tapped them on the desk. "You can't tell him about our arrangement. He wouldn't thank either one of us for making him our favorite charity."

"You didn't have to say it. I wish you hadn't."

"Thanks, Amos."

"It didn't turn out."

"Did you really expect it to?"

"I was in the zone. How's my credit?"

"Zero, officially. I'm still on probation. Unofficially, what can I do for you?"

"If you can spring my Luger loose from the Oakland County Sheriff's Department, we're square."

She wrote down the particulars, underlining Lieutenant Phillips' name. "I can't promise anything, officially or otherwise. We're not supposed to interfere with the locals."

"You can tell them it's all part of the Big Shuffle."

She called downtown, asking for Inspector Alderdyce. She listened, said, "Okay," and cradled the receiver. "You got a reprieve. He's out assisting the Grosse Pointe Police in a barricade situation."

I said, "I bet I know the address."

I couldn't get within a block of the place. A Grosse Pointe cruiser stood across both lanes of Lake Shore Drive and there were more cars parked in the street and on the lawn of the big house, all official, than when Darius Fuller's possessions were being auctioned off to pay his taxes. I gave a card to the uniform who came up to my car and asked him to give it to Inspector Alderdyce. He had me spell the name and told me to pull into the curb.

Ten minutes later he came back and handed me a temporary pass. I snapped away my cigarette butt, clipped the pass to my handkerchief pocket, and made my way through the spectators, sawhorses, yellow tape, and extra personnel to the miniature

328

version of the mansion in the backyard. The local armored squad had set up a firing perimeter ninety feet from the playhouse with shotguns and tear-gas launchers and bulletproof vans. John Alderdyce, wearing formfitting Kevlar under a beige poplin jacket, stood on the lee side of a van in conference with a Grosse Pointe commander with goldleaf on his visor. He broke off when I approached. The commander summoned over an officer in riot gear.

"Complaint came in from a salesman showing the estate to customers," Alderdyce told me. "Fuller snapped off a shot from inside when they approached the door. Commander Touhey says he fired wide, but Touhey put a sniper on the roof of the main house to wait for orders. Up here they make an effort to avoid gunning down baseball heroes."

I asked if there was a warrant out on Fuller.

"He has a room in an extended-stay place in Highland Park. We tried to serve it there, but he was out, probably by way of the back as the officers were knocking in front. Shopkeeper down the street from Hilary Bairn's apartment house came forward," he added. "He saw Fuller leaving just before we found Deirdre Fuller dead upstairs."

"It had to be that," I said. "Everyone else who looked good for it came up dirty on everything but."

"You look like you had fun eliminating them. I heard you found New York a little hot this time of year."

"I almost gave up smoking. Then I realized it saved my life. What happens to Fuller?"

"Deirdre was an accident. You can't plan a blow like that to be fatal. No jury would give him hard time. But he's endangering life and property from in there, and he's not responding to offers to negotiate."

"How do you know he didn't shoot himself or skeedaddle after he potted at the salesman?"

"He's in there, all right, and he's breathing."

I didn't question that, although a defense attorney would have. "What if I go in?"

"No civilians." Touhey had dismissed the riot officer. The Grosse Pointe commander was a hunk of weathered driftwood with a long Irish upper lip. "I'm not handing him any hostages."

Alderdyce said, "Walker's not a civilian. He's barely a citizen. And he's got a history with Fuller."

"So's his ex-wife. She's on her way here

from California."

"He'll be dead by the time she gets here," I said. "If your sharpshooter doesn't get itchy, he'll do it himself."

He chewed on that. "Will you sign a release?"

"If you like. There's no one to sue if your guy goes through me to get him."

"I know a couple of guys high up in the department who'd recommend you for chief if he does," Alderdyce said.

"Don't threaten me." Touhey signaled for a bullhorn.

"Piece." Alderdyce stuck out his hand.

I held up two fingers. "Peace, brother."

"Stop dicking around."

I smacked the Chief's Special into his palm and waited for my introduction to the man inside. No response followed.

It was like walking ninety feet naked on broken glass. They say it's the same running to first base. I stopped on the little porch, wiped my palm off on my pants, and tried the door. It wasn't locked.

"Close the door."

It was Fuller, sounding closer to eighty than sixty. He'd picked up a querulous tremor since we'd parted at his house on the lake, but that was natural enough. It seemed like twenty years ago.

I closed the door behind me. He was sitting on the floor with his back propped up against the far wall, bare now of trophies and pennants. He'd sweated through the black T-shirt he wore, and from the sour air in that shut-up building I figured he'd been sweating through it for days. His slacks were wrinkled and gray stubble sprouted from his chin. A nine-millimeter Beretta lay in his lap, loosely covered by his hand. It was plated in shiny nickel with mother-of-pearl grips, a lady's weapon.

"That the pistol you gave Deirdre?" I asked.

"She gave it back to me a month ago. She wanted to represent the antigun lobby when she got her license. Said it would be a conflict of interest."

Not reporting that had helped condemn Bairn; but that was ancient history now. "She give you the watch, too?" He was wearing it on his left wrist, a Rolex with a blue dial and a link band. I'd seen it before.

"She brought it to me here that day, looking for advice. I called her a stupid little slut, hanging around with a petty thief. That wasn't the way to handle it."

"You think?"

He ran a hand through his hair. It looked grayer now. "She ran out. I followed her. To apologize. When I saw where she was headed I got mad all over again. I shoved my way in before she could get the door shut. That's when she said she was going to marry Bairn right away." He smiled through the stubble. "It takes talent to get a woman madder at you than the guy she was mad at to begin with."

"That's all it was," I said. "It was the easiest thing to say that would hurt you back."

"I thought of that. Right after I hit her. Oh, God." He covered his face with his hands.

I tried for the gun then, but I wasn't standing close enough and he still had the reflexes of an athlete. He scooped it up and pointed it at me before I made two feet.

I let the tension go out of my muscles. "That's the third time this week for me, Darius. It's losing its effect."

He hesitated, as people will even when there's nothing else left. That gave me the edge. I kicked the pistol out of his hand as he moved to turn it up under his chin. He dived after it, no hesitation now, but I was too sore to get down and wrestle him for it. This time my foot caught him on the shoulder and he fell sprawling.

That was it for Darius Fuller. A good pitcher knows when it's time to leave the mound. He lay sobbing on the floor as I walked over and picked up the Beretta. I went back to the door and opened it just wide enough to throw the pistol out onto the grass. The troops moved in then.

If I had it to do again I don't know if I'd bother. The Detroit Police, who had jurisdiction in a city killing, put a twenty-four-hour watch on Fuller in holding, and the Wayne County Sheriff's Department took up the slack after he was transferred to the jail to await trial, but by the time the verdict came in he'd learned the futility of pausing even for a second. On the way to his sentencing for involuntary manslaughter, he wrestled his guard for his sidearm. During the hearing that followed, the guard couldn't testify whether it was his finger or Fuller's on the trigger when the gun went off.

Charlotte Sing vanished. The FBI and the U.S. Marshals raided her residences in California and Michigan and the offices of all her known businesses, removed truckloads of files and computers, and secured indictments against more than eighty coconspirators. Treasury froze all her assets. It didn't do much for the economy, and it didn't lead to the arrest of the central figure in the investigation, who'd been seen as far away as Nepal, wearing the robe of a Buddhist pilgrim, and as close as Toronto, dressed in the height of Paris fashion. Homeland Security placed her name on the list of international fugitives and advertised a reward of $100,000 for information resulting in her capture.

Darius Fuller survived the operation to remove a bullet from his thorax in Detroit Receiving Hospital but went into cardiac arrest in intensive care. He was buried in a private ceremony in Mt. Elliott Cemetery, eight blocks from where he grew up, wearing his 1968 World Series championship ring. I'd sent it to Gloria Fuller in care of the house on Black Squirrel Lake. It didn't go with my new suit.

ABOUT THE AUTHOR

Loren D. Estleman has written nearly sixty novels, this being the nineteenth one featuring Amos Walker. In his illustrious career in fiction he has already netted four Shamus Awards for detective fiction, five Golden Spur Awards for Western fiction, and three Western Heritage Awards, among his many professional honors. He lives with his wife, author Deborah Morgan, in Michigan.

We hope you have enjoyed this Large Print book. Other Thorndike, Wheeler, and Chivers Press Large Print books are available at your library or directly from the publishers.

For information about current and upcoming titles, please call or write, without obligation, to:

Publisher
Thorndike Press
295 Kennedy Memorial Drive
Waterville, ME 04901
Tel. (800) 223-1244

or visit our Web site at:

www.gale.com/thorndike
www.gale.com/wheeler

OR

Chivers Large Print
published by BBC Audiobooks Ltd
St James House, The Square
Lower Bristol Road
Bath BA2 3SB
England
Tel. +44(0) 800 136919
email: bbcaudiobooks@bbc.co.uk
www.bbcaudiobooks.co.uk

All our Large Print titles are designed for easy reading, and all our books are made to last.